THE LOOK OF LOVE

What happens when your impetuous step-sister goes on holiday to Italy engaged to one man, and then comes home with another? And not only that, but neither fiancé is aware of the other's existence! Before she knows it, Beth Tilney has promised to keep Lauren's double love life a secret — for now. And that's far from easy, especially when the Italian fiancé's cousin and best man, the intriguing and attractive Roberto Di Ferraio, arrives to keep an eye on things, and proves to be a big distraction . . .

Books by Marilyn Fountain
in the Linford Romance Library:

LEAP YEAR

MARILYN FOUNTAIN

THE LOOK OF LOVE

Complete and Unabridged

LINFORD
Leicester

First published in Great Britain in 2013

First Linford Edition
published 2014

A catalogue record for this book is available
from the British Library.

ISBN 978–1–4448–2154–3

Published by
F. A. Thorpe (Publishing)
Anstey, Leicestershire

Set by Words & Graphics Ltd.
Anstey, Leicestershire
Printed and bound in Great Britain by
T. J. International Ltd., Padstow, Cornwall

This book is printed on acid-free paper

1

That *must* be him. Lauren's Italian fiancé. Surely it could be no other; that colouring, that suit; that Latin attitude.

Beth Tilney, deliberately half-hidden behind a family group in the airport arrivals lounge, made no immediate move. She preferred to take a measured look first. She needed to familiarise herself with what she would be dealing with, gather some clues which might prove useful in the battle ahead — should it come to that.

She watched him saunter through the arrivals barrier — the relaxed, loose-limbed roam of a mature male panther — and then take a pause. Not in hesitation, not in uncertainty, not even in delay for his companion to catch up — although Beth knew she must be behind him because as yet there was no sign of her step-sister Lauren. No, he paused because this was a man who knew the impact his entrance into a room had on the females present.

There might just as well have been an announcement over the tannoy system: *Attention please; alpha male arrival at gate four. Will all casualties please proceed to the first aid station* . . . And he was right to expect the subsequent rippling effect, she couldn't deny that. Beth witnessed it with her own eyes. Ninety-nine point nine percent of the women in the arrivals lounge straightened their spines, flattened their stomachs, lifted their heads, raised hands to their hair.

The exception was Beth herself. Her chin was already lifted, but that was in preparation for the meeting. But as for all the other gestures . . . well, there was no use. Even if she was suddenly conscious that the long strands of her flyaway, soft-brown hair would be a tangled mess, as it always was five minutes after putting down a comb, and that the roots had flattened to her

2

scalp. She would have loved to give them a discreet lift, to smooth down the sides and tuck the ends under. Her fingertips were itching to do it, but she was determined not to give in to the urge, particularly for the benefit of a big-head who wouldn't give her a second glance anyway.

To resist temptation, she stuffed her hands deep into the pockets of her gilet, where they brushed a ball of twine and Major's spare leash on one side, and scraps of dirty paper and a pencil stub in the other. She looked down almost in surprise at it, and at the rest of her clothing. The gilet was covering a wash-worn, pink-checked cotton shirt, and skimmed the slack waistband of a pair of faded blue stretch trousers that had lost most of their oomph.

She remembered now, throwing on the first set of clothes that came to hand. Her gardening clothes were what she would have worn anyway today, until Lauren's pre-dawn phone call had whirled her into confusion before spinning her out on the mad dash to the airport.

Added up, it all meant that she was in no fit state to enter the competition to catch the eye of the jaw-droppingly handsome new arrival. But then she wasn't there to impress or attract him anyway, was she? And if what Beth's step-sister had breathlessly gabbled down the line was true, then he would be impervious to the charms of Helen of Troy, Salome and a whole troupe of sirens now that he had found the love of his life in Lauren.

Yet despite that there he stood, in a casually vigorous attitude, lapping up the female appreciation. Like the face of a flower tracking the sun, he probably couldn't help himself. And Beth had to admit — in her purely objective appraisal — that he was a physically impressive speci-men. Immensely tall, powerfully built, square-jawed, full and well-proportioned lips, glossed licks of blue-black hair swept back behind his ears. The only category she could put him in was as a model on the cover of one the novel-priced men's style magazines that occasionally turned up at the dentist's. Pity his eyes were hidden behind mirrored sunglasses. But of course they would be — all part of the image.

It was an affectation that Beth detested; sunglasses where there wasn't any sun. She mistrusted anyone who persisted in wearing them without necessity. It suggested they had something to hide.

As if he could read her thoughts, he removed the glasses — and looked straight at her.

She was caught red-handed, openly ogling him as if he were some blue-blooded stallion.

Beth froze, while simultaneously, conversely, a hot glow flooded up through her. The force that had earlier blown over every other woman now hit Beth alone.

The family group suddenly dissolved away, leaving her exposed. Everyone else faded to the fuzzy periphery of her vision. Despite being half an arrivals lounge apart, they could have been nose to nose. His eyes had caught hers and they wouldn't let go.

Of course they were Italianate dark, but no cold, coal-black chips, these. They were softened and warmed by the rich and sultry depth of Belgian chocolate.

With every pore Beth sensed danger; there had to be danger in eyes this expressive. For as surely as he was using them now to convey amusement, irony, triumph, a man so in tune with his physical self could effortlessly re-employ them as instruments of torture. And if she was struggling to withstand them now, how would she ever manage under other circumstances? What other circumstances . . . ? Her mind flailed around for coherence, but could find nothing.

All she could acknowledge, on a deeply instinctive level, was an immense, almost overpowering, sense of attraction.

He made the first move. If he hadn't,

she didn't know how long she would have been rooted there. But once he took a step forwards, somehow it released her too. And along with the movement came the crashing reality — and an appalling sense of shame. This was her step-sister's new fiancé, for heaven's sake!

As if the whole shock of that piece of news hadn't been staggering enough to hear in a five-thirty a.m. phone call. Beth could hardly recall the hectic dash to the airport though Monday morning rush hour traffic; her driving must have been on autopilot, while her mind was otherwise occupied in working, reworking, and rehearsing the approach she would take with Lauren.

And she'd finally determined exactly how she was going to handle this, which was to take command of the situation from the outset. Not in any heavy-handed way, but basically a steering job until the whole escapade blew over. Because surely that was what it would turn out to be. Lauren already had a fiancé at home here in England; and she had absolutely no business producing another one out of a hat!

Her step-sister was young, beautiful, headstrong — and a head-turner. Beth could well envisage Lauren turning the head of an immature Italian lad. And even how, swept up in the romance of a holiday atmosphere, the pair had mistaken infatuation for love. Taking the impetuous decision of getting engaged was clearly a step too far, but then that was the impulsivity of youth. Beth could understand that.

She'd reminded herself that she'd been nineteen once. Though in all honesty she'd never found herself engaged to one man, let alone to two and at the same time. Beth was only twenty-nine now, which was another fact she often had to remind herself of. But perhaps forgetfulness was only to be expected when she had so little time to devote to introspection. She was almost entirely consumed with the constant pressures and ongoing obligations of keeping the family home, Tilney Lodge, afloat. And trying to keep a stabilising hand on Lauren's unpredictable ways, of course.

Beth had begun to believe that Lauren's engagement to local farmer Ewen Walkis signalled a settling down. She'd been almost convinced it was one front at least on which she could relax. But now look what Lauren had done. Flown off alone on a prize short break to Italy — and got herself engaged to someone else!

At least Lauren was bringing him straight back home to Tilney Lodge to meet her; that was one thought that had consoled Beth on the journey here. That was a relief. A chance for the girl, and the boy concerned, to catch their breath and see sense. It could have been so very much worse. Some mad, whirlwind wedding in Rome, presented afterwards as a fait accompli. At home, Beth had reasoned as she'd driven up and down dozens of parking rows in the car park in search of a space, reality would set in. And she could gently but firmly guide Lauren and her equally idealistic 'fiancé' to see that it was all a flash in the pan.

The only, but crucial, crack that had opened up in Beth's strategy was staring her right in the face. Lauren's Italian fiancé wasn't the immature, infatuated youth Beth had anticipated at all. This man was too old, too experienced, too knowing, too sophisticated, too . . . too everything!

Her face flooded with another pulse of heat as her guilt turned to anger. If she had no business being attracted to him, then he had no business taking advantage of a naïve young woman who was already engaged to someone else!

Beth needed to make a lightning readjustment of her expectations, formulate a new plan, and give herself a good talking-to at the same time. And on top of that, just where, oh where, was Lauren?

She tried to gain a view around the

Italian as he loomed up towards her, but it was becoming increasingly impossible.

'Mr Di Ferraio?' she said, holding out her hand and tilting her head upwards. Beth was tall herself. But the more the gap between them diminished, the taller he became. He had two bulky brown leather travel bags hooked over his left shoulder. If they were as heavy as they looked, his posture made no concession to the weight. One black arm of the sunshades was suspended loosely from three fingers of his right hand.

'Beth.'

She expected him to transfer the glasses to his other hand in order to shake hers, to slow down, to stop — any second now. But he kept coming at her and, with a fluid, unhurried movement, both his hands came to rest on her upper arms and his head dipped to allow his lips to brush her cheeks in turn.

Beth stiffened. Deliberately. She had to. The delicate musky aroma of his cologne was so deliciously compelling. She inclined her head away both times, escaping the touch of his lips on her skin, but her evasion caused the pressure of his hands on her arms to increase. Through her cotton shirt she fancied she could feel the pattern of prints from his fingertips as they scorched into her skin.

Frowning, annoyed with him, but even more annoyed and appalled at herself, she pulled away and took a step back. And a very deep breath.

His expression, she noted, had not changed. Idle amusement, triumph, self-confidence: there they all were. But now she was this close, perhaps there was something else too. An alertness? A trace of wariness? Could her resistance, her failure to swoon, have surprised him? Good!

They spoke over each other. His English was very good, almost without accent, the tone as rich as his colouring.

'Beth. I've heard so much about you from — '

'Lauren? Where's Lauren ... ?' Beth's voice sounded squeaky and panicky to her ears.

He half turned, allowing her a view of the arrivals barrier. And as if he'd choreographed it to the very second, there stood Lauren, her wide blue eyes searching the people scattered there.

Beth raised her hand. Relief at seeing her at last, safe and sound, was tempered with confusion.

Lauren wasn't alone. A boy had his arm slung loosely around her waist, as her arm was around his. His wild hair was almost as long and curly and sun-kissed as Lauren's, though many shades darker than her wheaten blonde. Both wearing denim shorts, tee-shirts and flip-flops, they looked like a couple of carefree, gap-year, student backpackers.

Spotting Beth, Lauren shrieked a 'Hiya!', and, waving madly, lunged forwards. Her companion, still in tow, was almost dragged off his feet.

Beth blinked. If this was the fiancé . . . then just who was the Italian superstud? Acutely aware of his proximity, she stepped around him with exaggerated care. He'd known her name, he'd responded to the Di Ferraio name that Lauren had mentioned. There must be some connection.

'Beth!' yelled Lauren, who'd finally disengaged herself and was speeding over.

Beth's plans to play it cool suddenly sailed right out of the window. 'For goodness sake, Lauren, what on earth do you think you're playing at — ' But her tirade was halted by Lauren's effectively smothering her in a hug.

'Tell you everything later. Not now. Please . . . ' Lauren's pleading voice was just a whisper in Beth's ear.

When Lauren pulled away and back, Beth acknowledged her plea with an imperceptible nod. Perhaps it would be better to have it out in private once they were home, rather than in full view of the arrivals lounge, not to mention the

14

two Italians. The elder man in particular was paying very close attention, although his expression was unfathomable.

Beth glowered, a warning to Lauren that this was just a temporary reprieve.

'Thanks — ' Lauren blinked. ' — thanks so much for dashing over to collect us. This is Luca — Luciano Di Ferraio. Isn't he just as fabulously gorgeous as I told you on the phone!'

Beth appraised the now slightly pink-faced youth. Yes, he was rather gorgeous in a teenage pin-up kind of way. She smiled at him as a wave of relief swept through her. Because Luca was precisely what Lauren had led her to believe, and because she hadn't been fancying the new object of her step-sister's affection. For a second Beth felt almost light-hearted, as if she'd escaped from a yawning chasm opening at her feet. On safer territory now, and thankful to have finally reached it, her smile easily became a small laugh.

'Hi. Good to see you Beth,' Luca

said, in a voice which had much more of an Italian accent. When he stepped forwards to greet her with a hug and a kiss on each cheek, Beth relaxed and embraced him back.

'You too, Luca.' Relief made her response sound particularly heartfelt.

Aware of a movement of impatience from over her shoulder, she stepped back, half turning to the other man.

* * *

An enquiring glance at Lauren gleaned her nothing, and it was Luca who filled in the introduction. 'Beth, this is my cousin — ' he began.

'Roberto Di Ferraio.' The elder Di Ferraio displayed his impatience again by interrupting with his own self-introduction. A man unfamiliar and unsatisfied with not being the centre of attention, was Beth's summarising. Though she was none the wiser as to what he was doing here exactly.

She cast a brief, carefully gauged

glance in his direction, steering well clear from his eyes. She found herself wishing he'd put those sunglasses back on after all.

'We sort of introduced ourselves,' she told Luca, 'just before you and Lauren came through.'

'Roberto's going to be Luca's best man at our wedding . . . ' Lauren's distracted remark was an afterthought. The smiles she and Luca had gone into after the word *wedding* were gleeful and dreamy.

'What!' Beth spluttered, throwing a startled stare at Lauren. Wedding! Surely Lauren had brought Luca back to show him her home and to meet Beth, and to get to know him a bit better. At which point, in Beth's version anyhow, they'd soon realise it was all a rash mistake. Now she'd met Luca, Beth was seriously thinking that an engagement was an exaggeration. Luca hardly seemed mature enough to hold down a job, let alone ask a girl to marry him.

Even more now, Beth was convinced this was all Lauren's crazy idea. She pulled some surprises in her time, but surely even Lauren wasn't planning an instant wedding to Luca. But she must do, or why else should the best man have travelled over with them? Yet Lauren was due to marry Ewen Walkis in a couple of months.

Beth suddenly took in Lauren's left hand. Her *bare* left hand!

'Lauren! Where's your ring!' she blurted out, her own hand flying up to her mouth. Ewen's diamond solitaire was missing.

Lauren's eyes flashed with an unspoken plea for silence. 'We've not got around to a ring yet, have we, Luca?'

He shook his head dumbly.

Beth heard Roberto chip in with something about it all happening rather quickly. But she wasn't paying attention to him. She was stewing on the realisation that Lauren could not have even told Luca she was already engaged. Which meant she almost certainly hadn't told Ewen either. Poor Ewen. If the unlikely Italian romance did come to anything, he'd be devastated. How on earth could Lauren do this to him?

What a complete and utter mess. And no doubt one that Beth would have sort. She fired another hostile glare at Lauren, but it was like water off a duck's back.

Whether through lack of food or shock, Beth suddenly felt giddy. The whole situation was in danger of freefalling straight out of control. She was being steamrollered on all sides by all three of them. Lauren and Luca in their infatuated enthusiasm, and also by Roberto, standing there with such style and poise and self-confidence. Surely a man of his experience could see the ridiculousness of the situation? He couldn't possibly consider his teenage cousin marrying a girl of little more than a few days' acquaintance a good idea, could he?

But he must do, if he'd come to be

Luca's best man. She sneaked a sideways glance. He looked almost good enough to walk down the aisle as he was now. She pulled herself up sharp. There was her criticising Lauren for her recklessness, but was she any better, drooling over a man she'd only just met?

'Get a grip, Beth,' she muttered to herself.

'Pardon?' Roberto took a step nearer. 'I didn't catch what you said . . . '

She shook her head, trying not to breathe in another tantalising drift of cologne, and tried to focus on what to do for the best.

'Shall we go then?' Lauren said impatiently. 'It's okay for both Luca and Roberto to stay at the Lodge, isn't it, Beth? I've told them we have plenty of rooms.'

'Yes, okay then.' The best idea would be to go home. Sort it all out there. Stick to her original plan of allowing reality to dawn on the young idiots. Perhaps she could get the older Di

Ferraio on her side too.

Thank goodness Ewen was away on a course at the moment. Naturally he'd have to know all about Lauren's idiocy eventually, but it would only be added chaos if he turned up while Luca was there and the new engagement was still on.

'You are certain this won't put you to any trouble?' said Roberto Di Ferraio, who'd once again managed to position himself square in front of her.

A heck of a lot of trouble, she thought, her mind racing through the practicalities. She was terribly busy with the garden, and the businesses and activities contributing to the upkeep of the Tilney Lodge also needed her constant attention. Then there was Lauren's wedding arrangements. Lauren's original wedding, that was. Beth pressed her lips together tightly.

'You can't have been expecting two extra guests at short notice,' said Roberto.

'I hadn't been expecting one extra

guest,' she said pithily. 'But it's fine. You're both very welcome to stay, of course.'

Even if her teeth were gritted as she said it, what else could she say? The phrase 'embrace your enemy' came to mind. Though now she'd met him, not for a moment did she consider Luca to be an enemy. He was just a young lad, and apparently as romantically idealistic and foolish as Lauren. Whereas his cousin, Roberto — well, he was a completely different kettle of fish, wasn't he?

2

The young couple had linked up again and, with their holdalls over their free arms, were heading across the airport arrivals lounge towards the exit. Lauren was chatting animatedly and Luca gazing back adoringly.

Beth and Roberto fell into step behind them. 'I'm looking forward to seeing Lauren's home and the rest of the Tilney estate,' he said. 'Your sister has already told us a lot about it.'

Had she indeed? Beth hoped that Lauren hadn't bigged it up too much. The Di Ferraios weren't expecting some vast and palatial mansion, were they? Well it was too bad if they were. Roberto might wear expensive-looking clothes, but other than that, she knew nothing about him or his cousin. For all she knew, they could be a couple of confidence tricksters on the make. The idea seemed faintly ludicrous though, and Beth was smothering a grin as she replied, 'Let's hope you won't be disappointed then.'

'I've not been so far!' he returned, lightning-fast.

Beth glanced up at him, to find his head was already turned to her. His eyes fastened on hers before she'd thought to steel herself against their impact. Just before he switched them on to full 'knock 'em dead' mode, she glimpsed some other expression, but it was too fleeting to pin down exactly what.

Beth was feeling indignant, along with insignificant and on the back foot, as she carried on walking beside Roberto to the exit that Lauren and Luca had already gone through. Women were continuing to turn and stare at Roberto, after giving Beth a quick once-over and probably dismissing her as a cab driver or some other lackey. And who could blame them, dressed as she was.

Still, let people think what they like; why should it bother her? And she resumed pondering on what sort of impression Lauren had given the Di Ferraios about herself and her home.

As the exit doors opened automatically, Roberto hung back to allow her to go through first. He had impeccable manners. Was that all part of the act? Catching another heady breath of cologne, she gave his outstretched arm a wide berth.

Outside on the sunlit concrete, Lauren and Luca had their arms around each other as they waited. Beth tutted inwardly, and wondered if Roberto had heard it anyway when he also gave a small sigh.

'I feel rather like a Victorian chaperone, don't you?'

Was that amusement, indulgence or irritation? His tone didn't really give much of a clue, and she didn't want to risk looking straight into his eyes again.

She was squinting now anyway. 'The

sun's very bright,' she said, shielding her eyes and hoping he'd take the hint. The glasses were still dangling from his fingers. His nails were beautifully shaped and polished. A marked contrast to her own ragged examples. She thrust her hands into her pockets again.

'Here, take these!' He held out the glasses to her.

'No, I didn't mean you to — '

'I know, but really. Please make use of them, Beth. Here, allow me — '

Before she hardly knew what was happening, he was raising the glasses to her face, resting the bridge on her nose, lifting back her hair to hook the arms around her ears. But one side got caught up anyway.

'No — !' She jerked backwards, but he was nimble enough to move in exact time with her.

'Keep still, else it will only pull,' he said severely, proceeding to gently disentangle her hair. He was making rather a meal of it which, with hair as fine as hers, was totally unnecessary. If he left it, the glasses would simply slide out.

But she couldn't resist a proper peek at his eyes as he worked. They were so utterly beautiful. Up this close, she could see the tiny conker-brown flecks that softened the black. The thick glossy lashes with a minute upturned curl at the end of each one. Surface smile-creases radiated out below each eye like twin sunbursts. Imagining how the creases would deepen should he smile at her caused the blood to roar in her ears for a split second.

Beth blinked to cast off the dizziness and to escape his spellbinding eyes. Luckily Roberto was too focussed on the job in hand to notice the effect he had on her. Or perhaps it was such a common occurrence for him, such reactions became par for the course. Well thank goodness for that. One sister in the family making a fool of herself over a Di Ferraio was more than enough.

'There.' He smiled. Even his teeth

were perfectly white and regular. 'I trust I didn't hurt you too much. Let's try again.'

Again she pulled back, but he persisted, and this time succeeded in fitting the glasses on her.

'Hmm, too large for you,' he said, surveying her critically with his head on one side.

Regarding him through the shades gave Beth so much more confidence. She could see why he favoured them. But with or without sunglasses, Roberto's levels of self-confidence seemed undimmed.

'Your head is a lot larger than mine,' she heard herself saying.

'Hmm. Not the first time I've been told that my head is big,' he replied, a twitch of the lips indicating he was in on the joke.

Beth let her head drop to hide her own smile, and the glasses fell forwards, along with a lock of her hair. Roberto neatly caught the glasses, and smoothed back her hair.

'No, it's not going to work, is it? Oh, well, we tried,' he said, with an exaggerated sigh. 'But how will you manage to drive?'

'I've a pair in the car,' she said, wondering why she hadn't pointed that out in the first place. No doubt he was too . . .

'Hey, Beth!'

She looked across the concourse, almost in surprise. She'd all but forgotten about Lauren. Presumably she and Luca had witnessed the whole embarrassing sunglasses performance. Even now, a smirking Luca was speaking close to Lauren's ear.

'Which car park are you in?' called Lauren.

'Um, the short stay one, I think.'

Beth was relieved to be moving again. Roberto was pretty much full-on across a crowded room. In close proximity, she found him akin to some sort of electrical field that blocked normal, everyday functioning.

But her interlude of calm didn't last

long. Arriving in the car park, she couldn't remember exactly where she'd left the Toyota. Up and down the rows they went, with Beth feeling hotter and more embarrassed every minute.

'Are you sure you left it in this one?' asked Lauren, stopping mutinously by a ticket machine they'd already passed by three times.

'Yes!' Beth snapped. 'I remember that advertising hoarding on the fence over there.' It was for a lawn feed and weed treatment, and she'd thought how incongruous it was in a place that was wall-to-wall concrete, without so much as a dandelion in sight.

What she didn't remember was getting a ticket from the machine though. Still, it would be all right. She'd not been gone all that long.

The others had glanced at the advert now.

'She must be right,' Lauren said drolly. 'Anything to do with gardens always strikes a chord with Beth.'

Roberto remarked, 'Ah, the famous

Tilney Lodge gardens. I can't wait to see them.'

They weren't all that famous. What did he know about them? Beth wondered. Some more of Lauren's over-enthusiasm at work?

'But first we must find your car, Beth,' said Roberto, splitting away to wander off by himself. 'What model and colour are we looking for? Beth?'

'Er, it's a Toyota. Red. Reddish . . . ' Under the mud, it was red. She didn't want to draw more attention than was necessary to the scruffy, everyday vehicle she used. She was hoping to bundle everyone in and whisk them away without the new arrivals noticing too much. With Luca alone she might have got away with it, entranced as he was with Lauren. But there was no chance of getting anything past Roberto. He clearly wasn't the sort of man you could just bundle into a gardeners' pick-up.

Perhaps it would be better if they didn't find it. How much would a taxi to Suffolk cost? No, it was ridiculous; she needed her own vehicle to get around when she got home. And anyway, hadn't she determined not to bother impressing the unimpressable?

'Convertible? Saloon? Estate?' Roberto's dark brown voice carried clearly over the rows, but Beth decided to pretend she'd not heard.

Lauren's eyes had grown wide. She inched closer to Beth. 'What on earth did you bring the van for?'

'What do you mean? I've only got the van.'

'I thought you'd have come in my Mini.'

'I didn't give it a thought. You ringing up like that and I just — '

'But the van, honestly! It's such a disgrace . . . '

Beth felt herself bristling. 'Sorry if it's going to show you up, Lauren! But perhaps if you'd told me a bit more about who you were bringing home — '

'Okay, okay.' Lauren backed off. She clearly wasn't ready to explain anything until they were alone. But they were practically alone now. Luca was several metres away, relaxing on a low wall with his eyes closed, face raised to the sun. Clearly he was no help in a crisis. At least Roberto was making an effort. Several rows away now, but his blue-black head was still visible as he patrolled up and down.

'Lauren, you've got to tell me what's going on,' Beth demanded in a low hiss. 'What about Ewen? Have you spoken to him? Have you broken off your engagement — ?'

'Shush . . . shush . . . ' Lauren flapped her hands. Luca was loping across to join them, his hands in the pockets of his denims.

'Could this be it!' called a distant voice.

The trio squeezed through parked cars to where Roberto was standing, his suit jacket unbuttoned now to reveal a snowy white lawn shirt taut across a muscular chest, his hands on his narrow hips. It was a struggle to take her eyes off him, particularly when the alternative view was the sorry sight of her vehicle. She kept meaning to give it a wash, but it was a low priority job that just kept slipping down the list.

She nodded briefly. 'That's it. Great. Thanks.' She bit her lip as she fished in her pocket for the keys.

'Not so great, Beth. There seems to be a problem . . . ' Roberto was looking down at the nearside front tyre. Oh, no, not a flat!

When she rushed round to take a look, she discovered it was even worse. She'd been clamped.

A quick scan of the notice pinned to a lamp post told her it was a phone call and a fine before it would be released.

'You sort that out, Beth. I'll stay here with Luca. We can be putting the seats up in the back,' Lauren added pointedly.

'I didn't have time to do it before I left,' Beth protested. 'You phoned and I came running — ' As usual, she added to herself under her breath.

She unlocked the van so Lauren and Luca could organise the seating. Then, dragging her phone from the back pocket of her trousers, she rang the number and found herself listening to a message.

'I've got to go over to the admin block,' she announced.

'I'll come with you.' Roberto stopped prowling round the van like a caged big cat looking for a way out, and joined Beth.

'There's no need,' she told him. 'I'm perfectly capable.'

'I expect you are — '

She wondered why he'd paused. Then she realised. It was until he was out of earshot of the van — though not so far that he didn't have to lean in close to her ear to confide, '— but I don't want to be left here to play — how do you say? — the raspberry!'

'It's the gooseberry, actually!' A laugh escaped Beth. His English so far had been perfect and she had no doubt that he was familiar with this informal term.

But it was the fantastical idea of comparing Roberto with a soft fruit which was the killer.

'You think it's funny?' he said.

She squeezed the inside of her mouth between her teeth momentarily, so she could say with a completely straight face, 'Gone off the Victorian chaperone idea then?'

He took a rapid pace forwards in order to turn and face her, his eyes glittering mischievously. 'Why, do you think we need one!'

'Of course not!' She winced; that sounded so prissy and pathetic, but it was all she could think of to avoid letting him have the last word. 'And I don't need an escort to the admin block either,' she added.

Her rebuff had no effect whatsoever. He continued to stride alongside her, effortlessly keeping pace with her quick, shorter steps. In fact, she was speeding up to keep pace with him.

'Where is this admin block, Beth?' he asked.

'Oh, somewhere . . . ' She gazed around, looking for a sign, and finally catching sight of the building itself. 'There it is. Now perhaps you'll go back to the van and wait for me there. You can be putting your luggage in the back,' she added, noticing he was still burdened with the two bags.

'You're sure you can find it again?' he suggested without missing a beat.

If she were honest, she wasn't, not entirely, because she hadn't been concentrating again. But she attempted a dismissive toss of the head — which may or may not have succeeded in purpose. Roberto gave a shrug that could only be continental and turned to go back.

Beth opened the door to the office, only to emerge outside again just a few seconds later. Roberto was meandering his way back through the cars. Oh, rats, did she have to? But there was no alternative, other than to run after him and ask.

'Mr Di Ferraio! Roberto!'

He turned at her second call, despite it being softer and more reluctant than the first. He increased his pace a little to return to her, but without losing a microgram of poise or style.

'Um, I seem to have come out without any money on me . . . ' She was kicking herself for doing such an idiotic thing. 'They need a debit card payment before they'll send the mechanic to unclamp us. I drove here in such a rush, I never gave a second thought to my bag — '

The smile he gave her was so smug, it made her want to thump him.

Back in the admin office, Beth was still justifying her forgetfulness — more to herself than to him — as Roberto took out his leather wallet, chose a card and handed it over the counter.

The female assistant was simpering so much, Beth thought that Roberto could probably have charmed them out of the situation for nothing if he'd wanted to. After pressing the necessary buttons, the assistant returned his card along with the receipt, an apology, and an unashamed gaze of open admiration.

'It won't take very long for the device to be removed, will it?' a smiling Roberto raised his eyebrows at her.

Beth had seen the rules notice on the desk warning that it could take up to two hours.

Normal rules didn't apply to people like Roberto, she mused, as when they got back to the Toyota, the mechanic was already there and half-way though his job.

Finally, with Luca and Lauren already belted up in the back seat, Beth prepared to drive home. After stowing away one of his bags in the back alongside the two holdalls, Roberto held onto to the other one, which Beth could now see was a large camera case. So he was expecting to take some snaps while he was in England. Good idea. Hopefully that would keep him busy and out of her hair.

He folded his impressively large frame into the diminutive passenger seat with ease, but once there he spread himself out more comfortably, and expanded to fill almost every centimetre. The camera bag he tucked in the footwell, underneath his long legs.

Behind the wheel, Beth turned the key and mentally crossed her fingers. The engine fired first time. Now if only the gearbox was in a similarly co-operative mood . . .

'Just a moment.' Roberto's hand touched hers. 'Don't forget to put on your sunglasses. You'll be driving into the sun.'

She had forgotten. 'They're in the glove box.' She indicated with her head to his half of the dashboard.

'Yes,' he said, 'You'll need them.' He removed his hand away from hers and sat back. He even gazed pointedly out of the side window — despite the view being merely a row of parked cars — making no move whatsoever to retrieve and pass her the glasses. Not so exquisitely mannered now then!

She had to stretch across him to open

the drop-down door to get the glasses herself. And her hand would need to come perilously close to his legs to get underneath the door to slam it up again. 'Perhaps you wouldn't mind closing that,' she suggested, repositioning herself in the driver's seat, and putting on the glasses.

'Not at all,' he replied pleasantly.

Her sunglasses were only a flimsy plastic pair that had come free on the front of one of Lauren's glossy magazines, but she felt better with them on. A thin defence, but better than nothing.

Roberto had also put his mirrored shades back on too. That was two layers of defence now.

'And we're off!' Lauren chimed in from the back seat, which was the last word of general conversation they got from either her or Luca. The rest of the trip the couple spent murmuring to each other and then finally dozing.

Pulling out of the car park at last, Beth crossed her fingers and hoped for a hassle-free journey to the motorway. One with not too many gear changes. There was so little room between the gearstick and Roberto's right knee it was going to be all but impossible not to grab the wrong one by mistake. She'd have to keep a very close watch on where her hand was going. But at the same time she had to guard against her attention being caught by the blue-black gleam of fabric stretching tautly across his broad thigh.

3

The silence on the journey had reached deafening point, and Beth was casting around for some safe topic of conversation.

It would have to be directed at Roberto. A glance in the rear view mirror told her that Lauren and Luca had both dozed off. Lauren was never good with early-morning starts. They must have left Rome at first light. They both looked angelic. Luca's head, with his lion's mane of russet curls, was lolling on Lauren's shoulder. He looked even younger asleep. There was a trace of childlike petulance on his pouted lip. Lauren looked sweet, her round face with its smooth skin gently tanned by her few days in the Italian sunshine. She wouldn't be sleeping quite so easily if she knew it was with her mouth opened quite so unflatteringly. She was still very beautiful though, not that her looks or youth would save her from a good roasting when they got home and Beth could have some time in private with her.

Roberto must have caught her checking in the mirror, because he twisted in the passenger seat to take a peek in the back himself.

'Hmm. Butter wouldn't melt, hey! Isn't that the phrase? Butter. Gooseberries. Hmm . . . you English like your food, don't you?'

'I thought that was an Italian trait.'

He turned back again, but only so far. Now he was facing her, watching her drive. 'We treat it with respect, not just talk about it. We live to eat.'

'Perhaps we English prefer to live for other pleasures.' She felt, rather than saw, the slight raising of his eyebrows, and realised with a rush of blood to the face how what she'd said could be interpreted as innuendo. Did he think she was flirting or coming on to him? She hoped he didn't. She wasn't. It was taking all her concentration to keep this bizarre situation on any sort of even keel. It had just been the first response to enter her head.

She suddenly wondered if he was hungry. Her own stomach had grumbled a couple of times, but she was certain she'd managed to stifle the sound by holding in her stomach muscles very tightly. Ordinarily, good manners would have seen her asking if he and Luca wished to stop and get some food on the way. But then she would have had to ask Roberto for another loan of his debit card to pay for it, and that didn't seem very good manners at all. It had been humiliating enough over the clamping fee.

Which reminded her . . . Another glance in the mirror confirmed the two teenagers were still snoozing. She didn't want to give Lauren more ammunition to have another go at her. 'Thank you for lending me the car clamp money,' she said quietly. 'I'll pay you back as soon as we get home.'

'Thank you, Beth. Some English currency would be useful, save me rushing to a bank immediately.'

Just how long did he think he would be staying then? Dare she ask that? No, she decided. She wanted to keep her word and not get into any discussions without hearing Lauren out first. And that girl had better have some real good story to account for all this.

Peeling off the dual carriageway at last, Beth nodded towards the sign at the roundabout. 'Not much further to go now.'

She dropped down a gear for the Toyota to manage the incline. Once they'd reached the top, an impressive vista would open out. It was a favourite view of Beth's whenever she drove back this way. The rural English countryside in all its early spring glory. On the very horizon, though still invisible as yet, Tilney Lodge nestled behind a ribbon of trees, in front of which glinted a patchwork of small fields.

'Have you visited England much

before?' she asked.

'On and off,' he replied vaguely. 'Never this part of the country before though. It's very picturesque.'

'Do you live in the countryside?'

There was a small sense of surprise in the fleeting glance he gave her, before switching his attention back to the scenery. 'I keep an apartment in Rome. But our main home is in the country, yes.'

Our main home. Was he referring to him and a wife and children, perhaps? Beth felt a sting at the thought. He wasn't wearing a wedding ring. Surely any wife of his would insist on it! And he wouldn't keep a separate city apartment if he was married, would he? Unless his work was in the city. What was his work?

Perhaps he meant a Di Ferraio family home which he shared with Luca's branch of the family? Italian culture was very family-orientated, wasn't it? That was an altogether more comfortable thought than that of Roberto

47

complete with a beautiful wife and several cherubic bambinos. Not that it was any of her business either way.

Ah, but it might be, another part of her brain said. If Lauren and Luca did end up getting married, they would end up as part of an extended family; well, distant in-laws at least.

Beth was getting a headache with so much speculation. She took her hand off the steering wheel to rub her brow.

'Tired, Beth? Would you like me to drive the rest of the way?'

Roberto didn't miss anything, did he? 'No! Thank you, but no. We're nearly there now anyway. This is Shallingham, our nearest village.' She slowed down to far less than the maximum thirty, conscious of the school and the narrow pavement outside the parade of shops.

Local people she'd known all her life held up a hand in greeting as they recognised the Toyota trundling through.

The vicar, Kevin Eccles, was just coming out of St Edmund's lych gate.

It was the church where Lauren and Ewen were due to be married. Kevin had seen — or most probably heard — the van, and was hovering on the kerb, clearly hoping to catch a quick word about something or other.

This had the potential for disaster. Beth slowed, but with a deliberate crashing of gears, hoping it would wake Lauren and disturb Luca from her shoulder. But no, they were out for the count. In that case, they'd be better off staying put and not waking up half-way through. The vicar could get a bit long-winded at times.

She coasted to a halt, and wound the window down half-way. Hopefully the muddy portion would act as a bit of a screen. Luckily there were no side windows for rear seat passengers, so she might just get away with it. As long as this didn't take long.

'Hello there, Kevin, everything okay?'

'Yes, thank you, Beth. It was just a quick reminder about — oh!' Kevin peered past her and spotted Roberto.

'Oh, sorry, Beth, I didn't realise you had guests with you this week . . . '

Groaning inwardly, Beth made a rapid introduction, adding, 'Mr Di Ferraio is a family friend.' She was quite pleased with the description. It seemed to cover the situation without giving anything away. Whether Roberto would was another matter though.

'Very pleased to meet you,' said Kevin Eccles. 'Will you be staying for very long?'

There! It was as easy as that to ask the question. Beth turned to Roberto too. She was as keen to hear his answer as Kevin. But if Roberto said he was here for the wedding, she was in trouble. She caught a breath and held it.

Roberto's eyes flickered past hers. He'd removed the sunglasses to speak with Kevin. Just that little look in passing and she'd felt her stomach tingle. It was nerves, of course, in case he was about to give the whole game away.

'Hmm, not entirely sure, I'm afraid. My plans are still a bit undecided at the moment.'

Beth breathed again. Had Roberto sensed her panic, or was he as doubtful as she was about the commitment behind Luca and Lauren's engagement?

'Oh, well,' fluttered Kevin, 'I do hope you'll come and have a look round our little church if you get the time. We've a rather fine fifteenth-century rood screen and several other interesting treasures . . . '

'Then I'll certainly do my best to fit in a visit.'

Kevin looked delighted, and Beth was struck by how nice it was of Roberto to be so enthusiastic. The vicar was always trying to drum up interest for his church's most notable features. But then again, perhaps Roberto was genuinely interested in fifteenth-century rood screens . . .

'Perhaps you'll come along with Beth anyway . . . ' Kevin transferred his attention back to her. 'That's what I wanted to remind you of, Beth. Choir practice, tomorrow evening . . . '

Before she could respond, Roberto said, 'Oh, yes, I'd love to come along and hear Beth sing . . . '

Oh, would he! That's what he thought.

'Okay then, *I'll* see you tomorrow, Kevin . . . ' Beth said pointedly. She was on the point of pulling away. If it hadn't been for the inconvenient timing of a series of passing cars, she would have succeeded. But as she waited, her eyes impatiently on the wing mirror, Kevin suddenly remembered something else.

'Oh, Beth, I know what else I was going to ask you. Do you know when Ewen Walkis is due back?'

Beth froze. She involuntarily glanced in the rear view mirror. Lauren's eyelids fluttered. She'd woken but was sensibly pretending otherwise. Beth opened her mouth and closed it again. Luckily Kevin didn't seem to notice the rise in tension.

'Only I'm hoping he might have a vehicle that might reach up — ' He indicated over his shoulder to the church behind him. 'There's a problem with the guttering on the clerestory.'

'Er, no, sorry . . . oh!' In her eagerness to get away, her foot slipped on the accelerator and the engine gave a protesting roar. 'Sorry, I don't know exactly. But if he gets in touch, I'll ask him.'

'Bless you, my dear. Right, I'd better let you get on.'

Finally Beth pulled away and allowed herself the luxury of exhaling loudly, to which Roberto gave his own interpretation. 'He's not so very tiresome, your vicar, is he? Nice old chap, I thought.'

'Oh, yes, yes, Kevin's great.'

She felt almost light-hearted. That hadn't gone too badly after all. Luca hadn't stirred, Lauren was continuing to feign sleep, Beth had survived the mention of Ewen, and the vicar had been none the wiser. She might get stuck with Roberto at choir practice, but she felt sure he wouldn't really be interested enough in coming to that either. He and Luca could be half-way back to Rome by this time tomorrow . . . Her foot twisted off the clutch this time and the gear change crunched horribly.

Roberto cleared his throat.

If he was going to offer to drive again . . .

'So what is your choir practising for?'

'Oh, just a midsummer concert. It's held every year in the church.'

'And you sing every year?'

'No, this is my first year, actually. Kevin was desperate for some new recruits, so I said I'd have a go. I'm not very good at all.'

'I'm sure that's not true. You have a very tuneful speaking voice.'

Did she? She'd never thought about it. No, she was sure this was Roberto just being Roberto; flattery fell from his lips as easily as air.

'By the way, who is Ewen?'

The killer question was unexpected.

She'd thought she had gotten away with just the passing reference from Kevin. In the mirror, she caught sight of Lauren's renewed appeal for silence; a rapid blink and slight shake of the head. It confirmed her suspicions: Lauren definitely hadn't told Luca and his family anything about her English engagement to Ewen. Beth ground her teeth.

'Ewen?' she began. Her voice was hardly tuneful now, but more of a squeak. She cleared her throat. 'He's — um — a local farmer. He farms a few acres on what used to be some of the Tilney land. Before we had to sell it off,' she added, more to fill the silence than with any desire to supply the extra information. She waved her hand to vaguely encompass the small fields that could be seen through the gaps in the hedgerows they were driving past. 'Ewen can get hold of one of those cherry picker lift vehicles. I expect that was what the vicar was thinking of.'

Those were all perfectly true facts,

yet guilty heat from what she wasn't telling flooded her cheeks. After twisting round to take in the scenery, Roberto had turned back to look at her again. A few seconds of silence threatened to stretch on forever.

She guessed he suspected her of hiding something. She hated the thought of dishonesty and subterfuge with anyone, let alone this man who seemed to have the ability to see right through her, but what could she do . . . ? She'd given her word not to say anything for the time being. Beth wriggled uncomfortably in the seat. The sooner they got home and she could clear the air with Lauren the better.

Beth was overwhelmingly relieved to arrive at the penultimate bend in the road, even if the final gear change did result in her hand brushing against Roberto's leg. How annoying was that? — especially when she'd managed to avoid it every other single time. Ignoring the slip, she announced

56

briskly, 'Well, here we are then,' and turned into the gates and proceeded along the drive.

Roberto straightened up at last and peered eagerly out of the windscreen.

'It's not that big a deal,' she muttered, apprehensive that he was expecting something so much more impressive.

The house was in sight now, and despite her protestations of insignificance, Beth was incredibly fond and proud of it — and of the gardens in particular. She found herself on edge waiting for Roberto's response. Not that his opinion counted for anything specifically. But it was informative to get a first impression from a stranger. As they passed through the grounds, she tried seeing everything through his eyes, and became hypercritical because of it. Suddenly she was picking up on yew hedges that needed clipping, shrubs that needed attention, roses that should have been pruned by now. It was that untidy, in-between time of year, with the winter bedding well past its best. Some of the spring bulbs had already flowered, but the scruffy leaves had to be left standing to pour energy back for next year. And it was still too early to plant up the summer bedding pots and displays.

'It's charming, Beth,' he pronounced finally. 'Very traditional. Very English.'

'You should see it in June,' she replied without thinking. 'The garden shows its best then, with the roses out and the herbaceous borders in full flow.'

'I'd love to,' he said. 'Thank you.'

Taken aback, Beth stifled a gasp. He made it sound as if he was accepting a personal invitation, which wasn't what she'd meant at all. It was just a general remark.

'It's the perfect backdrop for a mid-summer wedding, I'd have thought.'

'That's what I pointed out to Lauren when she and — ' Beth stopped herself abruptly on the very edge of a sheer drop. When Lauren and Ewen were planning their wedding, she was going to say. That was due to take place at the end of June.

Had Roberto meant Lauren and Luca's wedding? If he thought he was staying that long he had another think coming! This whole double engagement mess that Lauren had gotten herself into would surely be sorted out in a day or two. Beth was convinced it was Ewen that Lauren really loved. And then it would be goodbye Luca, goodbye Roberto. They would never see either of them again for the rest of their lives. A sudden empty feeling yawned up from her stomach. It was lack of food, of course, yet her mouth felt so dry she couldn't contemplate putting a thing in it.

Beth pulled up the Toyota in a flurry of loose gravel at the side of the house. Lauren stirred with an exaggerated yawn. She nudged Luca in the ribs, and he came to lazily, slightly irritably, rubbing his eyes like a toddler.

Roberto sprang out and went round the back to open the rear doors. Beth joined him, to help with the luggage. The camera bag was already hoisted on his shoulder, and his suit, she noticed, looked annoyingly immaculate. If she hadn't known better, she would never have guessed he'd spent the last couple of hours squashed up and shaken to bits in a filthy old van. The mark of a good Italian tailor, she reckoned. She bet that suit hadn't come off the peg from a department store. Nor that shirt, or those shoes. All so impressive, or was that the intention — to impress? It could be all part of the image, of course. Were they genuine, or a couple of con men on the make? Just how much did Lauren really know about her new fiancé and his Italian stallion cousin?

Heat flooded her cheeks. Roberto had caught her staring again. She tossed her head, telling herself that he should be used to people staring. If he wanted anonymity, he should dress down, not look quite so stunning, shouldn't he!

The notion of actually telling him that to his face made her laugh privately to herself. She was still smiling as she took the holdall from Luca's hand. 'I'll take that, Luca.' She might not have issued the invitations, but he was still a guest in their home.

'No, allow me — ' Roberto already had his own bag and Lauren's, but managed to effortlessly take Luca's too.

'Hello Major! Have you missed me?' Lauren was stooping to welcome Beth's elderly chocolate Labrador, who'd emerged to greet the arrivals, but in his own good time. After having his fur ruffled by Lauren, he proceeded round the group. First Roberto, then Luca, and finally Beth. Typical. She was the one who did the feeding and caring, yet she was the last person on his list to get a greeting.

She fondled his ears lovingly. 'You old two-timer, you!'

Lauren gave her a rather scared glance, until she realised Beth was talking to the dog.

Roberto had taken all the bags to the door step, and was gazing around.

Did it meet his expectations? Beth wondered what he would make of the inside of the house. The upkeep was a continual work in progress. She knew the interior fell far short of the standard of the gardens.

At least she felt more confident now she was on home territory. Whatever either of the newcomers thought, she was going to take charge of this situation from here on in. And if Lauren thought she was going to disappear with Luca the minute they got in, she had another thing coming.

Beth led the way to the hall. It was oak-panelled, high-ceilinged, and with its ornate marble fireplace was easily the most impressive room in the house. And also the most convenient to get everyone sorted and organised as soon as possible. Roberto continued to gaze round, rather in the manner of a tourist, but without comment. Luca seemed dopey-eyed and still half asleep.

'I'll show you to your room first,' Beth told Roberto and Luca, leading them up the curved staircase, only pausing to throw down a stern glare at Lauren. Beside her, Major stood with his tail waving gently, but his ears at a confused angle. Familiar as he was to strangers coming and going, even the dog sensed these two latest arrivals had thrown a spanner in the works. 'Don't disappear, Lauren. I need a word.' Beth's casual instruction was fused with steel.

'I'll be in the kitchen.' Turning, Lauren sounded resigned as she headed through.

'Good idea,' Beth called, even though she was out of sight now. 'Put the kettle on, and see what food there is for lunch. I won't be long.'

On the landing at the top of the stairs, Beth turned left and along a short corridor until she reached the room she'd mentally designated.

'I hope you won't mind sharing . . . ?' If they did, it was too bad. She pushed open the door, and Luca and Roberto went in.

It was a large room, with two three-quarter sized beds dressed with crisp white linen and cream quilts. A couple of Victorian mahogany wardrobes stood in two corners, with a wide low matching chest of drawers in between. 'This is the only room that's made up at the moment. There's a private bathroom through that door.'

Roberto strode over to the window. 'What a perfect view,' he remarked.

And what perfect manners, she concluded to herself. Whether inherent or learned, he was far too polite to request a room each. Beth hesitated. She could have put herself out and prepared another room. She still could.

She glanced at Luca. He was listlessly unpacking his holdall. Roberto caught her gaze, and she read a silent approval there over the doubling up arrangement. She nodded imperceptibly, acknowledging his collusion.

It was the first firm inkling she'd had

that he could very well be as doubtful over the sudden engagement as Beth was. If he had come to make sure that his cousin didn't make some reckless mistake, then she and Roberto were really on the same side.

'Come down and have some lunch when you're sorted then?' she offered. And leaving them to unpack, she sped down to the kitchen to confront her step-sister.

4

Lauren was leaning with her elbows on the island breakfast bar, her fingers busy with the buttons of her mobile phone. Beside her sat a can of cola and a bag of crisps.

'Oh, Beth!' Lauren ran over and hugged her, then stepped back, her blue eyes sparkling, 'Isn't this just crazy!' She did a wild spinning dance, which ordinarily would have had Beth smiling. But not this time. She felt so annoyed, confused, dumbfounded, she hardly knew where to start.

'Lauren, I just can't believe this . . . What on earth do you think you're playing at — ?'

'No, I can't believe it's happened either. Isn't Luca just gorgeous.' Lauren wrapped her arms around herself, closed her eyes and turned on her heels. 'I never dreamed love would be like this . . . did you?'

'Because it's not love, you idiot, it's just a passing infatuation . . . ' Beth raged. She could hear herself: all her good intentions to stay calm and reasonable and let the romance blow itself out were long gone. She was too furious, too exhausted, too staggered. 'And what about poor Ewen in all this?'

At least Lauren had the decency to look crestfallen at her original fiancé's name.

'Have you spoken to him yet?'

'No.' She shrugged. 'Not since I've been away. If you must know, we had a bit of a bust-up before I went to Italy. He should have come with me, shouldn't he . . . ' Her voice, sounding less certain now, tailed off.

'How could he, when he was already booked on the forest management course?'

'Ewen could have taken his course a bit later on, couldn't he . . . ' Her tone rose defiantly again. ' . . . if he really cared for me?'

'He thinks the world of you!' Beth exploded furiously. 'He's doing it for your futures, Lauren. I think you only went to Italy without him to prove a point, and because you couldn't get your own way. But you've gone totally over the top and it just shows how immature you still are.'

'Oh, you sound just like my mother!'

'The stunts you pull, you make me feel like your mother! I don't think you're ready to settle down at all. Perhaps Ewen has had a lucky escape. And if Luca really does want to marry you, he's in for the biggest shock of his short life so far. No wonder his cousin has muscled in on the trip. I bet he's seen through you,' Beth added — or at least she hoped he had, 'even if Luca is too naïve to realise.'

'Oh, Roberto's a pussycat,' Lauren said airily.

Beth's jaw dropped. That was the last way she'd have described him.

'Luca can wrap him round his little finger.'

'Really? Like you can with me! I wouldn't be so sure with Roberto. Have you considered he might be doing exactly what I'm doing? Or I intended to do?'

Lauren stood wide-eyed, shaking her head.

'Just going along with it until the pair of you wake up.'

'Not going to happen,' Lauren responded sweetly.

'And what on earth did you tell them about this place? I got the impression Roberto was expecting the Ritz before he saw the reality.'

Lauren, turning pink, starting fiddling with her phone. 'I might have laid it on a bit thick, but I was only trying to impress Luca.'

Beth felt offended and mystified and annoyed. 'You shouldn't have to impress him with some invented background. It's good enough for Ewen, isn't it! But then you don't have anything to prove or pretend to him. He knows everything about you. He loves you for what you are, faults, ego and all, though heaven knows why, the poor man.' Beth shook her head in exasperation.

'Please don't keep going on about Ewen!' Lauren's face was flushing ever so brightly. 'I will tell him it's over, okay? And give him back his ring. It's safe in its box up in my room, so you don't have to worry about that either. But I'll tell him the news to his face. It's not the sort of announcement you make by text, is it!'

'Oh, you've got some sensitivity left then!'

'Please don't spoil it, Beth,' Lauren cajoled, catching hold of her hands. 'This is the most exciting thing that has ever happened to me. You've no idea what it was like, just to catch sight of someone and fall so utterly in love . . . '

Beth firmly pushed away the recollection of her first sight of Roberto at the airport. This wasn't about them.

' . . . it felt like stepping into a lift that wasn't there.'

'Yes, and you know what happens

then? You fall flat on your face on the floor. And then you wake up. Do you hear me, Lauren!' Beth's emotions had reached a peak. She wanted to shake Lauren until her teeth rattled. To resist the temptation, she paced up and down instead.

Lauren's eyes followed her. 'You're making an incredible fuss over something that's really simple, Beth, if only you could see it. It'll all work itself out, I promise you. Love always does in the end.'

Beth stared, unable to believe her ears. 'Oh for goodness sake . . . I wish you could hear yourself! And who can trust your promises? Certainly not Ewen, or me — ' Beth turned away to resume pacing, or she really would have swung for Lauren.

Poor Major had long ago retreated to his basket, with his ears firmly down. It was catching sight of them lifting again that alerted Beth to the fact that other people had entered the room.

Luca and Roberto were on the

threshold of the kitchen doorway. Luca had changed into calf-length cut-downs and a hooded sweatshirt, no doubt in response to the reduction in temperature. Roberto had changed clothes too. The obligatory camera bag was still over his shoulder, but now he was wearing black jeans and a checked shirt over a black tee-shirt. He might be dressed more casually now, but was no less devastating for it. The kitchen had suddenly become claustrophobic.

'Oh, you found your way down here okay then?'

How stupid was that! They'd only to follow the sound of raised voices. *Her* raised voice. Lauren was remaining beatifically calm.

'Yes, we found you,' said Roberto in a dry tone. 'It's not so large a house after all, is it.'

'No, it's not Buckingham Palace!' she snapped, more for Lauren's benefit. She squeezed her nails into her palms to calm herself. She had to stop rising at every turn. Hadn't that been the original plan at the beginning? The drive to the airport suddenly seemed a very long time ago.

Catching Luca eyeing up Lauren's crisp packet reminded Beth that she was supposed to be fixing them some food. Throwing her step-sister a look to tell her their discussion was far from over, Beth went to the fridge.

Lauren, meanwhile, had glided over to Luca and, after a brief murmuring together, announced they were going out. 'I thought I'd take Luca over to see Emma and Emily.'

'Well that's a good way of keeping him a sec- — ' Beth stopped, right on the point of blurting out about keeping him a secret. She gulped and started again. 'Is that such a good idea . . . because you've not had anything to eat yet.' Now she sounded more like Lauren's absent mother than ever, but it couldn't be helped. 'Neither of you,' she added lamely.

'No probs. We'll pick up a takeaway pizza in Allsham on the way,' Lauren called back over her shoulder as the pair left by the side door.

Beth was aware of a slight wince from Roberto. No doubt that was at the thought of a takeaway pizza. Great! He was a food snob into the bargain.

'Looks like it's just you and me then,' he said, making the situation sound unnecessarily intimate. Or was that just her interpretation? His voice, his smile, his eyes, they all made her knees wobble. She turned back to the fridge to escape. There wasn't much in there to keep her occupied though.

'Would a sandwich be okay? It's all I usually bother with in the middle of the day.'

'That would be fine.'

Slightly surprised, she responded, 'Oh, you weren't expecting four-course *cordon bleu* then?'

'Oh, six courses, at least!'

She gasped, but he was joking.

'But I'll cope with a sandwich.'

His smile was devastating.

'Um, cheese or ham?' she offered,

holding out the packets.

'May I — ?' In a couple of strides his long legs had crossed the kitchen. He pulled a face at the packet of sliced pink ham. She suspected the mousetrap cheddar only won out by a short whisker.

The only bread she had in was factory sliced white, the only spread was sunflower margarine. But he'd have to lump it. It wasn't her fault. She wasn't expecting to entertain, was she? She sneaked a quick glance. He was casting round the kitchen for something. Spying a wall rack of crockery, he prowled over and plucked out two medium-sized white plates.

'You don't have help around the house, Beth?'

'Staff, you mean?' She snapped it out. 'No. As you say, the house is only small, isn't it?'

He pursed his lips momentarily. A slight uncertainty at the reason for her curt tone. She felt a small quiver of triumph, quickly replaced by remorse.

It wasn't his fault if he'd been led to believe he was coming to some luxurious, fully-staffed mansion.

'We do have some part-time helpers that come in a casual basis now and again,' she amended, 'if we've week-long guests staying . . . ' He wasn't even listening. He'd gone back to the window and was scanning the outside view. 'Look, perhaps you'd like to take a wander round the grounds while I — ?'

'No. I'll stay.' He turned and came back to her with a smile on his face. 'And help if I may — ?'

'Really?'

'Yes, really, Beth.' He held out his hand. It seemed to hover in the air for a tremendously long time. For a crazy moment she was tempted to put her own hand in it and ask him to take her away with him. She shook away the delirium. Perhaps she was coming down with something.

Silently she passed him a spreading knife and the tub of margarine. Of course he didn't really want to be stuck with her in the kitchen, but perhaps he didn't trust her to make a simple sandwich.

'And you can show me round the grounds after lunch.'

She nodded, but with reluctance. She was hoping to get on with some work this afternoon. Especially after squandering a whole morning. And she didn't want to be stuck with Roberto all afternoon either. His presence was inhibiting, distracting. She was fumbling with opening the wrapper on the cheese now. All fingers and thumbs.

'Here — ' he said, taking it from her hands.

She watched his beautiful fingers find and tease open the seal. Luckily he didn't seem to notice her absorption, and merely passed the cheese back to her.

'So who are these people Lauren has taken Luca to see?'

'Emily and Emma. They're a couple of her old school friends. She'll be showing him off!' Beth said without thinking.

But Roberto laughed.

Beth was worried now. Should Lauren really be parading her new fiancé while her previous one had still to be told the news? Just as well Ewen was out of town at the moment. But this situation couldn't go on indefinitely.

'Roberto,' she began cautiously, 'this engagement has come as a bit of a surprise to me . . . ' That was an understatement, to say the least.

'Yes, it has happened very quickly.'

Annoyingly, his tone of voice gave no sense of how he felt about it. He was apparently absorbed in spreading the bread, but she noticed a small nerve was pulsing on the ridge of his cheekbone.

'Don't you think it's a — ?' She hesitated, before reformulating the question. 'Could Luca really be in love with Lauren — or — or — ?'

His shoulders appeared to tense, but

it could just have been associated with his next movement, which was to slide the breadboard towards her along the worktop.

'Or just in love with the idea?' Roberto finished her question. 'She is very beautiful, your sister — '

'Step-sister,' Beth corrected automatically, as she cross-cut the sandwiches and transferred them equally onto the two white plates, sliding one over to him.

'I didn't realise that.'

Roberto turned to look at her, leaning against the worktop while taking a bite of his sandwich.

Beth mirrored his pose. She felt better standing up too.

'My father remarried after my mother died. Lauren's my step-mother's daughter.'

Frowning, he straightened up and put the sandwich back on the plate. Was it the food or the turn of the conversation that had stayed his appetite?

He folded his arms and leaned again. 'So she's not your father's child?'

'No. Lauren was just a toddler when my dad married her mother.'

'You didn't mind? How old were you then?'

'Just turned ten. I'd always wanted a sister. I'd rather not have had to lose my mother to get one, but Lauren seemed like a sort of consolation prize . . . if you can understand that?'

'I think so . . . I, too, would have liked a sister or brother . . . although I have many cousins — like Luca!' He gave a wry look which made her want to smile. 'So does Lauren have any contact with her real father?'

'Never. Apparently he ran out on Lauren's mum before she was even born. She's had it tough really, poor kid.'

'Hmm, and not so easy for you either, Beth.'

Biting her lip, she shook her head wordlessly. Life had hardly been plain sailing. Her father remarrying had been a shock, and she'd fought hard to square her love for him against a sense of betrayal. She hadn't cried for ages about losing her mother so early, so heaven knows why tears threatened now. It could only be something about Roberto's understanding manner.

'So where are your father and step-mother now?' he asked.

'We lost Dad ten years ago, and Lauren's mum is in New Zealand. She's remarried again now.'

'Lauren did not want to go and live with her mother?'

'They never really got on that well.' Another understatement. Beth could still remember the blazing rows. Lauren's bedroom door was still warped from all the times it had been slammed so hard.

'Hmm, it's the way with mothers and daughters sometimes. Or so I understand. I have no real experience. As I said, I'm an only child.'

'Spoilt?' she said, not meaning to say it out loud.

He grinned. 'Probably!' He picked up the sandwich again and gave it an absent-minded glance before taking another bite.

'Still, it's a lot of responsibility for you, managing this place single-handedly and keeping an eye on Lauren, especially as she is no blood relative.'

'Well, no, but I consider her my sister in every other sense,' Beth said defensively, wondering if really he was fishing for information on Lauren's financial situation. Again, the wild thought flittered through her brain that the Di Ferraios could be a couple of scoundrels on the make, but it seemed just too ludicrous a notion to entertain for long.

'As far as I'm concerned, she's family,' she added.

'Ah, but surely you'll be having a family of your own, Beth. You'll want to marry and bear your husband many babies some day soon, I expect.'

It felt incredibly intimate, talking this way. If she'd been discussing this with a female friend, it would have been perfectly normal. But with Roberto, it was making her heart race.

Her warm face must be glowing like a post box. To give herself a bit of distance, she went to the sink and poured herself a glass of water. Unbelievably, he followed her. 'Good idea,' he said.

What was? Her marrying and having babies some day soon? But then his arm went up and plucked another glass from the shelf above the sink. And she exhaled, because he could only have meant that a drink of water was a good idea. To wash down the horrible sandwiches, no doubt.

'But in the meantime, Lauren continues to live here with you?'

'Of course!' Beth exclaimed in surprise. 'The Lodge is the only home she's ever really known. And it always will be for as long as she wants it to be,' she added. 'Not that she would have gone with her mother when she emigrated anyway. Lauren was in the middle of her A Levels at the time.'

'A Levels? She went on to university?'

'Oh, she went. But then she dropped out, I'm afraid.' It still disappointed Beth. That was another stunt that Lauren had pulled. Arriving home unannounced in the middle of her second term. That time, it was missing Ewen which had drawn her back.

'Lauren's intelligent, but — but — ' She wanted to say flighty, but drew back out of loyalty. 'That was why I was so pleased when she told me she was getting engaged — ' Beth stopped herself abruptly and in horror. Lauren's engagement to Ewen, she'd meant.

Roberto was just as dangerous as she'd instinctively known at first sight. There was something about him that invited confidences. But Lauren's engagement duplicity was her own affair, and as much as Beth decried her step-sister's deceit, it was up to Lauren to sort it out.

Roberto surveyed her thoughtfully, a

small frown creasing his broad brow. She couldn't begin to imagine what he was thinking.

'I can see why you're so protective of your little Lauren,' he finally said, 'but . . .'

'But perhaps it's time I let her stand or fall on her own two feet?'

'Perhaps that is exactly what she is —'

A tapping on the side entrance door halted Roberto and distracted Beth.

A middle-aged man's round face peered in. 'Beth, there's a problem — Oops, sorry, didn't realise you had company. I'll come back.'

Beth straightened up and took a few steps toward him. 'No, it's okay, Jim. What problem?'

'The marquee at the Yates' place. They're not happy about the position now it's up.'

'Really?' Beth sighed in dismay. 'I can't think why. It was all discussed at the quotation stage. But no matter, I'll go down and see what can be done. Thanks, Jim.'

She turned back, to find Roberto drying up the plates, cutlery and bread board.

'There was no need,' she chided gently, 'and we do run to a dishwasher.'

'For just a few things! Anyway, I like being a good guest.'

And he had been, so far. A very good guest. Putting up with sharing a room, and manfully soldiering through such a poor lunch which had effectively been little more than bread, cheese and water! And she still hadn't paid him back the clamping money.

'I'm not being a very good hostess, I'm afraid. Would you mind looking around the gardens by yourself after all? You could take a few snaps . . .'

'Snaps?'

She glanced at the camera bag he'd parked on a stool, and Roberto chuckled. 'Oh, yes, some snaps.'

What was so funny about that? Perhaps it meant something different in Italian? 'Only I'm going to have to go into Allsham on business,' she continued.

'You could show me Allsham instead,' he suggested, drying his hands. 'And I could take a few — er — snaps, there. If you don't mind company, that is?'

'It would mean another trip in the van again,' she replied doubtfully. Surely he couldn't face another one.

But apparently he could. 'Right, all done here,' he said, after restoring the dried and gleaming glasses to the shelf. 'Ready when you are.' The camera bag over his shoulder again, smiling, he held out his hand for her to lead the way back outside.

Beth had no option but to step forward in front of him, while silently cursing herself for not taking the opportunity to get changed into some better clothes while she was upstairs.

5

Beth got as far as the Toyota before she realised, and had to turn around and go back in. She'd forgotten her bag again. No excuse of an unexpected phone call this time. It was the Roberto Di Ferraio effect instead.

She considered nipping back up to get changed, but it would take too long. And besides, she didn't want Roberto thinking she'd done it for his benefit, did she?

Returning to the van, she was surprised to see her dog sitting in the back seat. 'Major, how did you get in there!'

'You don't mind?' said Roberto. 'Only he seemed to want to come.'

'Probably because he was left alone all morning,' said Beth. 'Did he get in by himself? He's got a touch of arthritis and finds jumping up difficult.'

'I gave him a leg up,' said Roberto.

She didn't know why that made her smile, but it did. Perhaps it was the growing realisation that he wasn't quite the arrogant, picture-perfect mannequin his appearance had led her to believe. He was happy to muck in, had humour and sensitivity . . . was almost human, in fact!

On the journey into Allsham, he asked why she was sorting out a problem with a marquee.

'It's one of the Tilney enterprises,' she explained, concerned that it sounded far grander than it actually was.

Her worry was compounded when Roberto's lips pursed. 'Hmm, Lauren mentioned you were an accomplished businesswoman.'

Beth almost snorted. Lauren again! Another disappointment for Roberto then, if he'd been expecting someone organised and crisp in heels and tailored suits.

'The marquee business came about by accident really,' she told him. 'I told you Lauren's mum remarried? The wedding took place here at the Lodge, and the elaborate marquee she wanted was so difficult to find we ended up having to import one from the States. So many people admired it and wanted to hire it from us, it ended up becoming a small business. The Yates family are using it for a big anniversary party this weekend.'

'So what are the other Tilney enterprises, Beth?'

'Weekend residential courses for one. History of gardening, the local landscape, that sort of thing. We get in expert tutors.' Her eye catching his camera bag under his knees again reminded her. 'Oh, we've run a couple of photography courses too.'

'Sounds interesting. You must let me know when you have the next one and I can come along.'

Beth opened her mouth to say there was one scheduled for the autumn, but who knew what would have happened by then. She was living from minute to minute at present.

'We also run a few murder-mystery weekends. They're popular. But garden tours are the main thing. There's been a recent development with that though.' Beth couldn't keep the excitement from her voice. 'The mother of someone who works for a television production company visited last year. She told her son, who came to look it over, and it's now on a list of outside location venues for film and television. It's already been featured in a costume drama. It was screened last month.'

'That must have been thrilling.' He smiled at her. 'Did it cause a lot of disruption? All those feet and all that equipment crushing everything. A lot of work for you to put everything back to order, I'd imagine.'

She nodded. It was true, and she was rather surprised that he'd picked up on that drawback. Mention TV or film crews to most people and they only thought of the glamour. But in reality, it was quite tedious and repetitive. The fee the companies paid was good compensation. What appealed to Beth most of all was having the gardens she'd known all her life and tended with such dedication immortalised on film.

Roberto had lowered the passenger window to peer at the same pretty patchwork of fields they'd passed on their way out of town earlier.

'Ah, this is the land that your family sold off? To your farmer friend, Ewen Walkis?'

'Yes,' she replied defensively. He didn't forget very much, did he? 'My father needed to raise some capital for essential repairs when he inherited The Lodge. He sold some land to Ewen's dad actually, but he's since retired and Ewen farms this portion now.'

'They are smaller fields than usual, aren't they?' he remarked.

She pulled up in a lay-by for him to have a better look.

'That's because he farms in the traditional manner,' she said proudly.

'He uses heavy horses instead of tractors.'

Beth loved what Ewen had achieved with his sustainable farming methods. She never minded knowing that the land had once belonged to the Lodge estate, when Ewen took such good care of both it and all the wildlife that subsequently flourished there.

'See that strip of forest over there?' She indicated to the horizon. 'It's an ancient woodland that Ewen is intending to restore. The coppicing will produce timber for traditional country crafts, for thatching and hurdlemaking.'

'And that's the training course he is away on at the moment?'

'Yes.'

Had she told him that, or had the vicar mentioned it earlier? She had the niggling feeling that Roberto and Luca may have overheard rather a lot of her and Lauren's kitchen argument. But in that case, surely Lauren's double engagement would have blown up in all their faces by now?

From the back seat, Major gave a huge yawn, before settling down and stretching out.

'Seen enough?' she asked Roberto, preparing to pull out into the road again.

'Yes, now I've familiarised myself with the scenery . . . '

Why should he want to do that, for heaven's sake?

' . . . just in case it should also feature in a future television show, and I can impress my friends and family by saying, 'Ah, I recognise that place!''

He was smiling again, and it was so easy to smile with him. So easy to feel happy as they bowled along past a row of ornamental cherry trees, fat with early pink blossom, the sun shining brightly through the van's windows — even if it did show up the appalling layer of dust and muck. So easy to forget the Lauren situation and just enjoy his company — if enjoy was the word. She was still on edge in case she should let something slip, but then perhaps that gave an extra edge to the sensation. And if it wasn't for Lauren's crazy behaviour, she would never have met Roberto Di Ferraio. Would never have known he existed.

How weird and uncomfortable a thought that was. That they would have been alive at the same time, him in his part of the world, and her in this one, but could have lived out their whole lives and never met. She suddenly shivered.

'Cold?' He instantly began winding up the window. 'Are you okay? You suddenly look very, very serious. You have an unpleasant thought? You shouldn't, Beth, not on a day like today. No-one should. You should be happy. Just like I am right now.'

Was he really? She sneaked a look. Yes, he seemed contented enough.

'Aren't you, Beth? What's wrong?'

What was wrong! She didn't know where to start, and if she did, she couldn't tell him anyway.

'Nothing. I was just thinking about

serendipity. Fate,' she clarified. 'About what a mysterious thing it is.'

'Do you believe in it?'

Did she? 'I'm not sure. Probably. Doesn't everyone, deep down? Do you?'

'Most definitely. I mean, just look at us. We wouldn't be here together without it, would we?'

She shook her head. With the road ahead straight and clear, she put her foot down on the accelerator, and decided to concentrate on the happy for now.

Roberto suggested he take a sight-seeing stroll around Allsham, while she sorted out the marquee business.

'I hope you won't be disappointed, it's only a very small town.'

'Oh, I can usually find something of interest in most places. And Major can come with me,' he added, as the dog had stirred the moment Beth had parked up just off the main square and switched off the engine. 'Save him getting lonely and bored.'

'Well, if you're sure,' replied Beth. She pulled the lead from her pocket. Roberto took it, clipped it onto Major's collar and gently helped the old dog from the back seat. She found it a touching sight.

With Major safely on the ground, Roberto turned and caught her staring. His eyebrow raised quizzically, and Beth altered her expression. 'Shall we meet back here in, say, thirty minutes?'

'Fine with me.' He hesitated for a brief instant before adding, 'At the risk of sounding like a typical Italian man who thinks of nothing but his appetite . . . are there any plans for dinner this evening yet?'

There weren't. She'd been wondering, and worrying, over what on earth she could offer them. When the Lodge had course guests staying, she either ordered in ready-made food in advance, or the catering firm she used would bring in their own in-house dishes. 'We could eat out . . . ?'

'I'd be happy to cook, Beth, if you'd allow me?'

It sounded great, but it felt wrong, awkward. 'You're supposed to be a guest,' she protested, but only half-heartedly. Witnessing Roberto in the kitchen earlier made her suspect cooking was a particular skill of his.

'Look, Beth, Luca and I have been sprung onto you at the last minute . . . '

She liked the diplomatic way he didn't bring up Lauren as being responsible for that.

' . . . I can't expect you to have plans in place to cater for us.'

That was true enough. And she still had no idea how long they would be staying, did she . . . ? Suddenly the circumstances came crashing into her brain and began whirling again.

How long would it take Lauren to realise she was making a mistake? From their conversation earlier, it didn't seem as if it would be in the very near future. Perhaps Luca might have second thoughts. Had Roberto really come along expecting to be his cousin's best man? No, it was ridiculous. He could only have come along to put the brakes on a rash wedding.

She'd much rather allow herself to believe that they were on the same side. Was it total madness to think she could even enjoy having such a charismatic house guest for a few days . . . ?

'I don't like to brag, Beth, but I have been told I'm rather talented in the kitchen . . . '

She raised an eyebrow.

'Admittedly by my mother! But if you'd take a risk on an Italian mama's judgement, I'd be happy to rustle something up.'

'Okay, you're on,' she grinned, because her stomach was rumbling already, and she found herself wanting to please him. But hadn't she warned herself against doing just that a few hours ago? She shook the annoying inner voice away. 'I'm looking forward to it already.'

'Now I'm worried in case my recipes

don't pass muster!' He gazed round the small square. 'I'm hoping there's a good delicatessen around here somewhere.'

Beth smiled and pointed. 'Just down that side lane.'

'We'll see you later then. Come on, then, boy . . .'

Roberto strolled away at Major's sedate pace. She watched the combination for a while; her old dog that she'd known and loved since the day she'd clapped eyes on him as a seven-week old puppy, and the man that she'd only met this morning.

And something in her heart went ping. It worried her. Something new and exciting and scary was happening, and she didn't have a clue how to react to it.

The business with the Yates' marquee was thankfully quickly sorted to the family's satisfaction, and Beth was first to arrive back to the market square. Where was Roberto? Still at the deli, or taking some snapshots of the town? Remembering the money she owed him, she headed for the wall cash dispenser outside the bank.

She'd just withdrawn the notes when he turned up, Major loyally at his side. She'd devised a way of not buckling whenever she looked at Roberto now. It meant never looking full on into his eyes, but focussing elsewhere on his face. It wasn't foolproof. He was so stunningly handsome that wherever she looked there was still an impact. But it meant she could function fairly normally. Whatever must it be like to be his girlfriend?, she speculated wildly. No, she told herself firmly, don't even go anywhere near that scenario.

'Good timing,' she said lightly. 'Here's the money I owe you from this morning.'

'There's no need,' he said, making no move to take it.

'Please. I don't like being in anyone's debt.'

'Okay then, thank you. But tell you what, let's spend it on wine to go with tonight's feast — ' He held up two bulging carrier bags.

'What on earth are we having?' she asked, wide-eyed.

His head dipped to hers. 'Ah, wait and see. It might be your English chips and eggs and beans!'

Somehow she doubted it. In the wine merchants, she stood and daydreamed while Roberto discussed and selected his purchases. A wine for every course, by the sound of it. She went light-headed after a single glass of cheap plonk. It would have to be a small sip of each for her, otherwise she could end up making a complete fool of herself.

Roberto passed her one of the other bags, so he could carry the wine. 'What's in here?' she said, looking down as they left the shop. 'Smells like delicious fresh bread — '

'That's because it is. I found an artisan bakery a few streets back.'

Beth turned to him. 'Is there? I'd no idea. Yet I've shopped here all my life.'

'Perhaps for things other than food,

Beth,' he suggested gently. 'You dash round a supermarket for that . . . '

His tone was teasing and so were his eyes. She was ready with a quick retort, except she'd forgotten her golden rule and met his gaze head-on, and the words fell from her mind. His eyes dropped to her lips and —

'Hello, Beth! Small world!'

She turned to find a couple in their sixties almost upon them. Already they were gazing at Roberto with undisguised curiosity.

'Oh, hello!' she chirped, forcing brightness into her voice. 'This is Roberto Di Ferraio, a family friend . . . ' She was getting quite accomplished at this now, wasn't she, she thought as she completed the introduction. 'Derek and Pam Meadows. They used to run Shallingham Post Office and newsagents.'

Roberto placed the bags carefully on the ground in order to shake their hands. After saying their hellos, the older couple fussed Major briefly before returning their attention to the new-comer.

'Do I detect a European accent, Mr Di Ferraio . . . ?'

Beth could hardly believe it of the sensible, no-nonsense Pam Meadows she knew, but the woman was actually fluttering her eyelashes.

'Roberto, please. Yes, I'm from Italy.'

'Oh, we've had some smashing holidays there, haven't we, Derek . . . ?'

Before Pam could really get into her stride, Beth apologetically suggested that she really had to get on. But it still sounded abrupt and she felt incredibly guilty.

'Busy as ever, Beth,' smiled Pam. 'And now what with all the wedding arrangements on top of everything else . . . '

Beth steeled herself for the sky to fall.

' . . . you're over here a bit too early for that though, Mr — er — Roberto. No doubt you'll be returning in June . . . ?'

Confusion fell on Roberto's face. As

well it might, winced Beth. She must get him away before the Meadowses unwittingly gave the whole game away. What would he think if she tucked her arm through his and dragged him away down the street?

'We thought we saw Lauren drive past in her little Mini,' Derek chipped in, 'and wondered if you were — '

'Yes, I believe Lauren was coming into Allsham earlier . . . ' Beth interrupted, on the principle that if she talked, they couldn't. 'She had some friends she wanted to see and . . . '

'That's right, Derek, I'd forgotten,' Pam interrupted back. 'We wasn't sure if it was her though because we couldn't see you or Ewe- — Oh, Beth, are you all right?'

Beth had had no alternative but to develop a sudden coughing fit. Major gazed up at her curiously. Roberto, with remarkable speed, sprang to her aid by patting her on the back. That was a remedy the medical boffins hadn't tested. Roberto's touch. It 'cured' Beth instantly. Although it did set off a chain reaction of other symptoms, especially as his hand was still resting gently against her back, burning its way through her clothes.

'Okay now, Beth?' he asked, after the Meadowses had continued on their way. 'Do you need a drink?'

'Wine!' she exclaimed, alerted by the chinking of glass bottles as he picked up the carrier bags.

'Of course, if you'd like some. But wouldn't water be better?'

He was laughing at her. He knew full well that her coughing fit wasn't genuine. Beth tried to recover her dignity along with her diminishing integrity. It wasn't until they were back at the van that Roberto remarked, 'They weren't so very bad to chat to, were they, that you had to develop a rapid case of bronchitis to escape?'

'No, no, of course not. The Meadowses are a nice couple. I just didn't want to stand there chatting all day. I've got things to do back home,' she added brusquely. She was still disturbed by her reaction to his touch.

Shopping, dog and Roberto in the van, Beth switched on the engine.

'Or — ' Roberto added, his voice low and husky, ' — could it be that perhaps you wanted to bustle me away because you felt uncomfortable being out and about with me . . . ?'

Her hand was on the gearstick, and he placed his gently on top. Heat flowed up her arm.

That was even more shocking than his words. But he didn't really think that, did he? In a way, of course, he was spot on. If only she wasn't tied to keeping Lauren's secret, she'd be only too happy to be seen with a man like Roberto. Happy — and incredulous that he'd want to be seen with someone as scruffy and unsophisticated as her!

Not daring to meet his eyes, biting her bottom lip, she shook her head.

'Sorry,' he said, his head dipping closer. 'I didn't hear that.'

'Of course not,' she whispered. 'What a ridiculous idea!' But she was the ridiculous one, wasn't she? In danger of falling completely for this man's natural flirtiness and physical charms. What did she know about him really?, she reminded herself. Absolutely nothing.

With supreme effort, she pushed the gear into reverse. It crunched horribly. But his hand was still curled over hers. 'Only I wouldn't care for that thought at all, Beth. It would hurt me very deeply.'

Behind them, a car pulled up and indicated, waiting to take the space she was about to vacate.

'Then please don't think it,' she told him, 'because it's really not true.'

'Then I'm satisfied — ' He removed his hand, straightened up and leaned back in the passenger seat. Beth took a breath. It felt like being released from a spell, and she couldn't decide whether she should feel relieved or bereft.

' — for now,' he added, which sent

her stomach tumbling into yet another wave of cartwheels. What on earth did that mean?

When they got back to the Lodge, Lauren's Mini was still missing. 'No matter yet. Plenty of time before we eat,' said Roberto, unpacking the bags in the kitchen as if he'd lived there for years. 'But I need to make a start on some of the dishes. Yes, a little something may come your way shortly,' he teased Major, who was sniffing round the bags, investigating the delicious aromas. 'If you're a good boy!'

Beth felt a bit superfluous and wondered what she should do. There was paperwork to deal with in the office, and jobs in the garden. But the whole day had turned out so differently to what she'd been expecting. It felt like a holiday now. She was seriously tempted to take a long bath, and spend some time getting dressed up into something more flattering for the evening meal. But it was far too early for that.

'Unless you need me to help, I'd better get on — ' She indicated towards outside, half hoping he'd ask her to stay.

But he didn't.

'Please, don't let me interrupt your plans any more. I can find my way around the kitchen. I'll bring you out a coffee when it's ready,' he said, already eyeing up the espresso machine she hadn't bothered using for months.

* * *

'Ah, there you are, Beth.' It was twenty minutes later that he brought her out a mug, Major at his heels.

She jumped a little. 'Oh, thanks.' She'd become engrossed in the work, dealing with several large clumps of delphiniums, trying not to trample over their tender shoots as she fitted staking frames around them.

'It has to be done now,' she explained. 'Then the stems grow through and look perfectly natural later on.'

He'd put her coffee down on one of the terrace steps, and held out his hand to help her out of the herbaceous border.

She tried to blow her untidy hair out of her eyes and face. Her hands were filthy, as usual.

'Allow me — '

He reached out with the clear intention to smooth back her hair, but she was ready for him this time, and determinedly moved backwards to brush it back herself, using the back of her hand. 'It's fine — '

He gazed at her, shaking his head. 'Now you have dirt on your face.' He stepped forwards. She couldn't go any further backwards without toppling over the wall by the steps or standing on the edging rows of bright green alchemilla mollis. Were they worth the sacrifice?

Her brain seemed incapable of working. She was like a hypnotised animal as his fingertips gently moved around her eye, her cheek and then to the side of her mouth. Surely her own hands had gone nowhere near there!

'There!' he exclaimed, standing back and admiring his handiwork. 'Normality restored. Now, drink your coffee. I must get back to the stove.' With a wink, he turned and strode away.

Major went to follow, but she called him back. He came reluctantly, and sat and leaned by her legs, but his eyes followed Roberto.

So did Beth's. Roberto was so — so — overwhelming attractive. And the coffee was absolutely gorgeous as well. He must have bought some freshly ground from the deli. He really was a man who thought of everything.

Beth decided she must get a grip and gather her thoughts. She was still furious with Lauren, who had yet to arrive back from parading Luca around her set of friends. Her step-sister wasn't answering her phone; either she'd left it in the car or was deliberately ignoring her. Beth left a message and got on with some more of the gardening work she'd been planning to do that day.

It was only simple pruning, tying in and tidying. It wasn't worth starting on any complicated transplanting jobs that wouldn't get finished before dusk. But even the simple tasks proved problematic today. It was because her routine had gone out of kilter. She felt out of kilter. The afternoon was drawing in now anyway.

After putting away her tools, she went in. There were some amazing smells coming from the kitchen, to where Major headed immediately. Beth didn't want Roberto to think she was checking up on him, but she had the excuse of taking back her coffee mug, didn't she?

He was measuring out ingredients when she crept silently in the door. But he immediately seemed aware she was there. He looked up and smiled lazily. A now almost-familiar jolt went through her.

'Finished for the day?' he asked.

'Outside, yes.' She nodded towards

113

the office. 'But there's always paper-work waiting.'

She wandered over to the stove. Every saucepan in the place was apparently employed with something or other. She peered inquisitively into a few. 'This all looks complicated,' she said, twiddling with a wooden spoon in one of them. 'Anything I can do to help?'

'No, no.' He sped over to her and, with his hands resting lightly on her arms, steered her towards the door through to the hall. 'It's all under control. Just relax, Beth . . . '

Relax? With all this going on? Well that just wasn't going to happen, was it!

6

Beth woke up, confused for a moment in the darkness. Where on earth was she? She groped for the bedside lamp, and when the light flooded the familiar surroundings of her bedroom, it all came back to her. She'd come up to her room to ring Lauren in private, and to shut her eyes for a second.

The clock said twenty past seven! She'd been asleep for over an hour. And she couldn't even say she felt any better for it. Befuddled and dopey, she headed for the shower, wondering how Roberto was getting on in the kitchen. He must be tired too. His start would have been even earlier than hers. What time was dinner supposed to be? Hopefully not until eight. That would give her a bit of time to do something with her hair and think about what to wear. Admittedly, the latter wouldn't take very long.

Sitting down in front of the mirror, Beth checked her phone. Typical, no signal, as there so often wasn't inside the Lodge. She composed yet another text, insisting Lauren bring herself and Luca back in time for dinner, and pressed send. As expected, it went straight to the Out Box and sat there. Once she was downstairs, she'd have to remember to go outside, where the signal was usually strong enough for it to work.

Beth picked up her hairbrush and sighed at her reflection; pale, heart-shaped face and high cheekbones — they weren't bad, admittedly. But she wished her eyes were more dramatic, more defined. Her father always said rather proudly that she had the typical Tilney North Sea eyes. In her opinion, that meant changeable and wishy-washy. Tonight they seemed to be greyish-green, rather than the bluey-green she preferred. Still, there was nothing she could do about it! She'd be better off focussing on something she could improve.

Typically it was one of those times when her hair would do everything but go the way she wanted. However much she tried to make the ends tuck smoothly under, they insisted on sticking out at odd angles. Perhaps a little make-up would prove a distraction. She never usually bothered but tonight she felt she needed it, to hide behind and give her a bit of confidence.

Where was her make-up? She rattled through the drawers in the dressing table. She'd not seen her small make-up bag for ages. But Lauren was bound to have some that she wouldn't mind letting her use.

Slipping out of her room, she glanced along the corridor. What timing! Because there was Roberto, making his way along from the opposite end of the corridor, heading for the stairs. He'd changed back into his suit trousers, and a clean white shirt. He looked stunning. Beth began inching backwards. Perhaps if she was

very quiet and still, he wouldn't notice
her —

'Oh, there you are, Beth.' He
stopped, his hand on the banister. His
dark eyes flickered up and down. Beth,
feeling like the hapless guest in his
home, was acutely conscious of the
shabby old dark blue towelling robe
she'd thrown on.

'Dinner in fifteen minutes. Would
that be all right . . . ?'

His expression, she noted, was
doubtful, as well it might be. He was
probably thinking she'd need fifteen
hours to make herself presentable.

Beth straightened up and said coolly,
'Yes, perfectly all right. Thank you,' she
called after him, remembering that he
was doing all the cooking after all, but
he'd already jogged away down the
stairs.

Feeling rattled, Beth picked a lipstick
from among Lauren's large collection
and went back her own room. The
decision over what to wear wasn't
difficult. The only thing remotely

suitable was her sage green silk dress. Knee-length, with a swirly skirt, cross-over top and three-quarter-length sleeves. It wasn't new, but it seemed to complement her colouring. Thrusting her feet into a pair of cream slingbacks, she headed downstairs, and straight for the dining room.

Roberto had been busy. The table had already been set. He'd even found and put out the slender white candles.

'Everything meets with your approval, Beth?'

She started, not realising he was behind her. 'Yes,' she gulped, turning. 'I was just going to get the table ready, but it seems you've thought of everything.'

He was staring at her, taking in her dress, her face, her hair — and probably thinking that for all the time she'd had to get ready, she still looked a sight.

Roberto smiled, and reached for her hand. 'You look lovely, Beth,' he said softly.

She bit her lip and gave a self-conscious murmur of thanks. Did he mean it? Or was he just being charming and gallant. She liked to think she presented a slightly more feminine and attractive image than she'd done so far today, but was sure she fell far short of the type of sophisticated Italian women he was used to.

She reminded herself of her own earlier advice at the airport, and shook herself to. She wasn't in the competition to catch the attention of Roberto Di Ferraio, was she? All she was doing was acting as a host for a surprise guest until Lauren came to her senses and the infatuation fizzled out.

'I can't think where Lauren has got to,' she frowned, side-stepping Roberto, and wondering if she could catch Lauren for a few more words in private before they all sat down together. 'Have I got time to take Major round the grounds to stretch his legs before dinner?'

'Good idea! The food's all in hand. It

only needs to be served. So I'm able to come with you.'

He would be, wouldn't he! She was excited and thwarted in equal measure.

'It really is a beautiful garden,' he remarked, as they strolled down the drive at Major's dawdling pace. Dotted here and there in the borders were solar lamps, but the moon was full and so clear and bright it provided ample illumination without them.

'Moonlight helps,' she said. 'It puts a silver lining on everything and veils over all the unattractive bits.' Hopefully it might do the same for her, Beth thought wryly.

'I see no unattractive bits,' said Roberto.

'You've not had the chance of a proper look yet.'

'Oh, you'd be surprised!' There was a small smile playing on his lips. Beth quickly looked away again.

'I had a wander round with my camera this afternoon.'

'Did you? I didn't notice.'

'You were busy working. I took a few — what do you call them? — snaps. I hope you don't mind.'

'No. No, of course not.' She didn't really, but she would have preferred to have pointed him towards the garden's best features. Roberto might be one of those people who liked to photograph scruffy or shabby under the guise of it being 'arty'. 'I'd love to see them,' she added.

'Of course, Beth. I was going to ask if I could use your computer to load them up to my website anyway.'

'Be my guest. It's in the office just off the kitchen. Do it after dinner, if you like.'

'I'd like to email the pictures to my mother too. She admires the classic English style of gardening very much. At home, she's the gardener in the family. Ours is on a slope, so it's a series of terraces by necessity. Not so many flowering plants as this, though she's planted many different types of shrubs and small trees to create a wonderful effect. There's a tiny spring too, which has been channelled into stone rills, so that each terrace has its own miniature waterfall . . . '

'Sounds lovely,' she murmured. The moonlight was making her feel dreamy, that and listening to his rich-toned voice and imagining this beautiful Italianate garden.

'I should love you to see it, Beth,' he said, which brought her to with a jolt. But it was just conversation, wasn't it? Unless Lauren and Luca really were in love and ended up getting married . . . was that really possible?

Poor Ewen. Beth frowned. He adored Lauren. It would break his heart.

They were at the entrance gates now. No sign of Lauren's car, or any other vehicle on the quiet country road. It was incredibly rude and self-centred of her not to turn up for dinner. Beth dithered. Should they wait, or go back in and start without them?

Beth shivered in the chilly breeze. She should have popped on a jacket, but then Roberto had come out in just his shirtsleeves.

'You're getting cold,' he said, folding his arm around her shoulders. Warmth flooded through her. 'Should we go back inside, Beth?'

'I think we might as well,' she said, although it had been on the tip of her tongue to say that she was perfectly content to stay exactly as they were.

Inching herself free of his arm, she bustled up Major, who'd been rootling around in some hedging, and pointed him back towards the Lodge.

* * *

'This has definitely been Lauren and Luca's loss,' she remarked, after Roberto had served a pasta starter, fish for the main course, and a meringue dessert. The wine he'd chosen, a different bottle for each course, had been perfect too, though she'd limited herself to a small glass each time. She'd made enough of a fool of herself today, without ending up stumbling around or — heaven forbid — blurting out how gorgeous he was.

'You really enjoyed it?' he asked.

She risked a look into his eyes across the candlelit table. He seemed genuinely uncertain and curious.

'I've cleared every plate you've put in front of me,' she replied lightly.

'Ah, but that could be because you are very polite.'

'It was only my politeness which stopped me from licking them all clean and demanding seconds!'

Laughing, he pushed back his chair and began gathering up the plates. 'We could be greedy and eat the other two dinners.'

Beth, standing up too, gave a small groan. 'That would be too much of a good thing. I really couldn't manage any more.' She collected up the wine glasses and cutlery.

In the kitchen, she loaded the dishwasher, while Roberto made two small cups of dark espresso. Beth led the way back to the little snug. She wished she'd had the foresight to light the fire, but with all the table lamps lit, it was still reasonably cosy but without looking too intimate. Roberto settled in the centre of the sofa with a satisfied exclamation of contentment. Major, who'd trundled through with them, stretched out on the rug at his feet. Beth took another look at her phone. The text message had gone at least, but the signal strength indicator was flashing unreliably.

'Still no word?' he asked, indicating her to sit on the cushion beside him.

Lips pressing together, she shook her head as she settled into a small side chair instead, then immediately wished she hadn't. It was hard to avoid his direct gaze from there. She'd have been better off sitting beside him after all. But she couldn't swap seats now without him thinking she was crazy.

'Little madam! I'm sure she's avoiding me.'

'Like you're avoiding me?' he said.

'No — ' Beth faltered, taken aback at his question and kicking herself for speaking aloud her thoughts about Lauren. She just knew Roberto wouldn't let it pass — and he didn't.

'Why would Lauren be avoiding you?'

Yep, no escape from those dark eyes, boring into her soul. The idea of sharing her concerns with him was tempting. She couldn't tell him the full story, but it made sense to sound out exactly where he stood on the situation too.

She took a deep breath. 'Because Lauren knows I'm not too pleased over her sudden engagement.'

Roberto leaned forwards, his forearms pressing onto his thighs. 'No? At the airport I had the impression that you were very delighted to meet her new fiancé.'

'Did you?' She paused, frowning. Perhaps her greeting of Luca had seemed wholehearted, but that was mainly in relief on discovering that he wasn't the alpha male she'd been ogling! But she wasn't going to admit that to Roberto.

'Naturally, I'm worried that they're making a mistake. They're both so young, and they've not known each other five minutes. It's all happened so quickly. Surely you must have the same concerns?'

He was silent for a couple of seconds, as if weighing up his response.

'Actually, yes, of course I do,' he admitted, his shoulders noticeably relaxing. 'In fact, my role of best man is a bit of a cover. It seemed a good excuse to come along and keep tabs on them.'

Beth exhaled in relief. 'I guessed you had to be as worried as me, and were just going along with the idea until they came to their senses.' She only wished they'd had this conversation several hours ago; it would have saved her a lot of anxiety.

'I wasn't convinced that was your take on it though, Beth,' he was saying. 'News of the wedding seemed to have spread before we even arrived.'

Beth's mouth opened and closed again. He was thinking of what the Meadowses had said. What he couldn't know was that it was Lauren and Ewen's wedding that the couple had referred to. But she couldn't say anything until Lauren came clean about it, and decided which of her fiancés she was going to commit to. If any, after this! Beth rubbed her forehead in consternation.

'They can't possibly really be in love, can they?' she said. 'Lauren and Luca, I mean. Not after so short a space of time. I've not even had a chance to ask her how they met.' Nor do I know the first thing about your cousin or you, she wanted to add, but made sure she didn't say that aloud.

'It was at a photographic exhibition in Rome,' he said. 'Their eyes met across a crowded room. Isn't that the expression?'

She nodded distractedly. 'You were there?'

129

'Yes.' He relaxed into the sofa again. 'It was a rather large event, packed with people. One minute Luca was standing around, apparently rather bored, the next he was chatting with the beautiful blonde girl who turned out to be your step-sister.'

Who chatted who up? Beth suspected it was more likely to have been Lauren making the running.

'I didn't actually catch the magical moment it was supposed to happen.'

'It . . . ?' Uncomprehending, she gave a little shake of her head.

'The moment they supposedly fell in love,' he explained.

Supposedly . . . ? 'You don't believe in love at first sight then?'

Roberto blinked. He actually blinked. She'd faced up to his eyes, and he'd looked away first. She felt a small surge of triumph, while at the same time was hanging on tenterhooks for his answer.

She watched him smooth an invisible piece of fluff from his trousers. 'No, I don't,' he said.

Why on earth did that feel such an enormous let-down? She was of the same opinion, wasn't she? That love at first sight was the fanciful concept of fairy tales and romantic stories.

'An overwhelming attraction at first sight . . . ' he said, glancing up, his gaze back on full force again, 'now that's perfectly credible. But how often does it indicate true love, or even that true love will follow . . . ?' His voice tailed off.

'Even if it might feel like the real thing at the time?' She heard her small voice fill the silence that drummed in her ears.

'Ah, but that's the secret, isn't it? Knowing the difference.' His voice had softened and lowered too, yet his powerful eyes still kept her captive.

It was the strangest moment, akin to teetering on the edge of a cliff-top. Time had stopped and Beth felt as immobile as a statue, yet the barest movement could send her world spinning. She desperately wanted something to happen to break the spell.

In the end it was Roberto, clearing his throat and reaching for his coffee. 'What I do believe,' he said, taking a couple of sips, 'is that Luca is immature and doesn't know his own mind. This week he's in love with idea of marrying Lauren, next week he's liable to want to start a rock band, or become an astronaut the week after.' He shook his head, smiling ruefully. 'I'm sure I was the same at his age.'

Beth picked up her own coffee. 'Which did you want to do when you were his age?' How many girls had thought themselves in love with him? That was what she really wanted to know. Or perhaps she didn't. The answer was probably in the hundreds!

'Me? Actually, I fancied myself as a bit of an artist at nineteen.'

'Did you? The next Michelangelo?'

He pursed his lips, considering. 'Hmm, more like a misunderstood Van Gogh. I ran away to Paris with nothing more than an easel and a paintbrush, intending to starve in a garret for my vocation.' He pulled a dramatic expression which made her laugh.

'So what happened? Lack of money?'

'Lack of talent,' he replied succinctly. 'My paintings were truly awful. What I saw in my head just wouldn't translate onto the canvas. So I went back home and took up photography instead.'

'Not space travel then, or rock music, or — or — breaking hearts?' She couldn't resist steering him back to that.

'Not knowingly,' he said, pulling a face at himself, 'but what do I know. Perhaps women are fainting at my feet as I pass and I just don't realise it!'

It was so close to her first snap analysis of him, that Beth almost gasped. She was revising her opinion of him by the minute. He was not at all the big-headed, self-obsessed egoist she'd had him down as; he was turning out to be funny, kind, practical and perfectly prepared to take the mickey out of himself. Who would have guessed he was any of those things when she'd caught first sight of him across the airport lounge?

Perhaps it should serve as a warning against making snap judgements on first impressions. They could be equally as deceptive and unreliable as the falling in love at first sight fantasy.

Falling in love . . . ? Is that what she was doing? If she was, then she'd better stop it. So what if she had discovered his character and personality were just as attractive as his physical attributes? If anything, it just made her feel even more outside of his league.

Beth shifted to the edge of her chair so she could briskly pick up her coffee cup and saucer. 'Shall we go and get a refill, and then load up your photographs on the computer?'

Roberto blinked, as if taken aback by the sudden change of atmosphere, but he got up and followed her from the room.

Taking fresh cups of coffee into the office, Beth gave the desk chair to Roberto, and she pulled up a spare chair alongside him — but making sure it wasn't too close.

He loaded up the memory card, and soon dozens of photographic file icons littered the screen. 'That many?' she exclaimed. 'I thought you'd only taken a few.'

'That is a few for me,' he replied. He clicked open the first one. It showed Beth sitting on the step with Major by her feet. Her head was at an angle and she was clearly saying something to the dog, whose head was raised to look at her.

She squirmed uncomfortably. She never liked seeing herself in photographs, and particularly when caught unawares and looking such an untidy mess.

'You don't like it?' he asked.

'Not much,' she muttered.

He leaned in to scrutinise it more closely. 'I'm rather pleased with it. Technically, it's very satisfactory. Good composition, nice balance of figures and background.' He sounded rather hurt.

'Sorry,' she muttered. As he was clearly such a keen photographer she should have realised he was talking about the technical aspects of the shot, and that he would be sensitive to criticism. She'd feel exactly the same if anyone questioned the way she structured the garden.

'It's not the shot,' she clarified, 'more your choice of subject. Major looks great,' she added, but realised it was too little too late.

'Never mind,' he said, getting to work with the mouse, 'there are plenty others that might appeal more.'

There were indeed plenty more, though to her eyes none any more pleasing than the first. Beth featured in every single one, either absorbed in work, or taking a breather and merely standing and staring into apparent space with a perplexed expression.

'I'd no idea you were taking any of these at the time.'

That pleased him. 'Ah! A good photographer should be invisible. It's the way to get the best shots.'

If these were the best, she'd hate to see the worst!

Deftly wielding the mouse, he began grouping several photographs together. 'I'll email these to my mother tonight.'

'Perhaps you should wait and take some more in the morning,' she suggested. 'Some which actually show the garden, rather than me?'

He turned — not just his head, but shifted the chair too, twisting it ninety degrees and so sat facing her.

'But you are the garden, Beth. Yes, it's a beautiful, romantic, traditional space, with its intricate patterns of plants and flowers, colours and texture. But to include the person who's lovingly created it, tends it and nourishes it, that is what gives the pictures their strength. You and your garden, Beth, are irrevocably linked in my mind.'

Her thoughts began to gather, and words — objections mainly — began to form, but the mechanism stalled when she realised his head was moving towards her. His eyelids lowered. His hands were gripping the arms of his chair, but she felt herself being drawn towards him by some invisible impulsion. Her own eyes were transfixed by his lips. She just knew, without a shadow of a doubt, that he was going to kiss her. She was longing to feel his lips on hers, yet the prospect scared her too. She felt so totally out of her depth. She should move away. She should stand up and walk out of the room. But she didn't really want to. And there was no way her legs would hold her up.

She closed her eyes.

His kiss, when it came, was restrained, cautious, rather questioning, and very, very sweet. Just the merest pressure of his lips on hers. How could she have felt scared. It was so beautiful. And she wanted more. Dare she respond — ? Could she stop herself!

Her hands were just on the point of reaching out to curl around his neck — when a sudden clatter came from the direction of somewhere beyond the kitchen, rapidly followed by the click-clack of Major's claws on the flagstones.

Beth's eyes flew open, her hands dropping into her lap. Roberto drew back slowly.

'That must be Lauren and Luca . . . ' she murmured, ' . . . at last. Thank goodness for that!' She scrambled up, wobbled a bit, but recovered by gripping the back of the chair for support. And it was thank goodness they were back, wasn't it? Because not only had she been anxiously waiting for them all evening, but their timely arrival could very well have prevented her making a total fool of herself with Roberto.

He'd stood up too, and was shutting down the computer. 'Perhaps I will come back to this in the morning,' he said. 'I'd like a few words with Luca, and I'm sure you want to talk to Lauren . . . '

' . . . Beth . . . Beth?' Lauren's distant voice grew closer.

She was about to leave the office,

when she felt his hand gently cup her arm. 'I've enjoyed this evening, Beth, very much . . . '

She turned. *Don't look at me like that*, an inner voice was screaming in her head, *because it just makes me long to be kissed again.*

'Yes, me too . . . '

'And we're united now, aren't we?'

She blinked wildly. 'United?' she breathed.

'Of the same mind about the engagement? We just sit it out and wait for the fever to pass.'

'You make it sound like a case of flu.'

'Perhaps that's exactly what infatuation is like . . . '

The office door, which was ajar, swung wide open, and the young couple walked in.

'Here you are!' exclaimed Lauren. 'It was like the *Mary Celeste* everywhere else in the house, wasn't it Luca?'

Luca, looking blank-faced, gave a shrug.

'We wondered whether you'd gone

out to eat after all,' added Lauren.

'No, we didn't. And you've missed a fantastic dinner . . . Roberto cooked,' she added, in response to Lauren's raised eyebrow.

'Did you leave anything for us? I could eat again,' said Luca, 'the food at the hospital was not good.'

'Hospital!' Beth heard Roberto's exclamation echo her own.

'Keep calm,' said Lauren. 'Emily's grandad was in for a heart operation. There were complications while he was under the anaesthetic and she was in a right state. So we decided to take her up there and keep her company while she waited for news.'

'You decided,' remarked Luca, sounding sulky.

'She's my best friend. And she needed me.'

Was this a sign of the very first crack in the romance? Beth couldn't help feeling sorry for Luca; it would have been a dull evening for him. But typical of Lauren's warm heart to want to be there to support her friend. If Luca really loved Lauren, he wouldn't have minded, would he? She sneaked a quick glance to see if Roberto was making the same analysis, but his neutral expression gave no clue.

'So how's Emily's grandad now?' asked Beth.

'Out of danger, thank goodness. And once she'd had a chance to see him, we dropped her off home and then came straight back here.' Lauren suddenly yawned. 'Wow, I'm so tired. I think I'll go straight up to bed.'

'I thought we were going to watch a DVD?' objected Luca.

Roberto stepped in. 'Take pity on your aged cousin! Watch it tomorrow, yes? I don't want you crashing about later and waking me up.' With a brief 'goodnight', he all but herded Luca through the door and towards the stairs.

'Sorry I didn't call,' said Lauren, when she and Beth were alone. 'I had to switch my phone off in the hospital, and couldn't use it when I was driving back.'

'Okay,' sighed Beth. She was building up for another confrontation with Lauren, but feeling far from sharp enough for the task right now. 'I suppose that means you've not spoken with Ewen yet either?'

'I told you I was going to leave it until I saw him.'

'It might all be over between you and Luca before then.'

Lauren whirled round. 'No. Why should it? What on earth makes you say that?'

Beth wished she hadn't. She'd been thinking aloud again.

'I don't know,' she sighed. 'Perhaps because I sensed a less than harmonious atmosphere between you and Luca just now.'

'He's just tired,' Lauren said lightly. She suddenly grinned. 'My mates think he's fabulous though.'

'Oh, well, that's the main thing, isn't it!'

'Oh, stop it, Beth.'

'No, you stop it, Lauren. I've tried to be reasonable and go along with this — frankly — quite crazy engagement of yours. But it's deceitful and wrong. I had a chance of a quiet chat with Roberto earlier and — '

'Hmm . . . ' Lauren's eyes gleamed mischievously. 'I thought you looked very cosy in here together.'

Lips still tingling, the kiss replayed in Beth's head. She hoped her cheeks weren't glowing as brightly as they felt. 'We were only looking at the snaps of the garden he'd taken earlier . . . '

'Snaps!' Lauren chuckled. 'I hope you didn't call them that to his face.'

'I can't remember now. Probably. Why not?'

'Why not?' She blinked rapidly. 'Because he's only one of Italy's top society portrait photographers!'

Beth felt a horrible sinking feeling in the pit of the stomach. 'You're joking . . . ?'

Lauren shook her head.

'I assumed he was just a keen amateur. He told me you and Luca met at a photography exhibition . . . '

'That's right. An exhibition of Roberto's work.'

'Oh!' Beth gasped. At least it explained Roberto's focus on her rather than the garden. It was his professional instincts coming to the fore. No particular interest in her personally. Of course not. Thank goodness she hadn't thrown herself at him and kissed him back. She felt foolish enough without adding that to her growing list of faux pas.

'Why on earth didn't you tell me?'

'You haven't exactly given me much of a chance . . . I know, I know . . . ' Lauren forestalled Beth's protests. 'Most of that is my fault . . . ' She broke off and yawned again. 'I really am totally bushed. Can't we talk about this in the morning?'

'Oh, go on,' Beth relented. 'Get to bed then.'

'Thanks, sis.' Lauren gave her a quick

hug before wishing her goodnight.

Not much chance of that, thought Beth, not least of all because of that disturbing kiss. But she was grateful to have some time to herself at last. It had been a non-stop day, even before the latest revelation about Roberto Di Ferraio. Could he really be a famous professional photographer?

However tired she was, there was no way she would rest without knowing that. Sitting down at the desk, she switched on the computer and typed his name into the internet search engine.

Website after website came up, detailing his career, his exhibitions, and examples of his work. There was page after page of the famous beautiful women he'd photographed, from film actresses to pop stars to European royalty. One site gave Roberto Di Ferraio's biography, which included his age, 38, and his marital status, single. Several articles came up linking him romantically with his more famous sitters, but even Beth — who was no expert on celebrity journalism — could recognise speculative story-making when she read it. But then she came across a piece regarding his family background. And that was the biggest eye-opener of all.

The Di Ferraio family was practically Italian aristocracy.

An image of the aristocratic Roberto materialised in front of her. It explained a lot about his natural bearing, authority and confidence. None of that was acquired in five minutes; it was either bred into you or instilled from birth. Luca had it too underneath, though it was largely masked at present by teenage attitude.

Almost on autopilot, Beth carried out her usual bedtime routine of settling Major in his basket, checking the locks and switching off the downstairs lights, before making her way up. All was quiet from the guest-rooms end of the corridor. She peeked round the door of Lauren's room; her step-sister was dead to the world, her golden hair spread

147

over the pillow like a halo, her face relaxed in carefree sleep. Did she know all about Luca's distinguished family heritage too? Of course she must.

Beth hardly remembered undressing and cleaning her teeth. Wearily she climbed into bed, knowing that sleep would be unlikely. Her mind was too active, going over the day's events, trying to recall every conversation.

She cringed inwardly when she remembered speculating that the two Italians could be a couple of scoundrels. How wrong she'd been on that! Lauren was the one with everything to gain by marrying Luca. She could be coming across as a right little gold-digger . . .

Beth sat bolt upright up in bed and gasped aloud. Of course! That was the real reason Roberto had come, to check out the Tilneys. It explained his curiosity about Lauren's place in the family. He was clever, wasn't he, making Beth feel as if he was interested in her life, when all along he'd been pumping her for information. He'd not come out and said he thought the engagement was a mistake until he'd dug out everything he needed to know — and made his mind up that Lauren just wasn't good enough for Luca!

7

When Beth dragged herself out of bed her eyes felt as if they'd been sprinkled with sand. And her head was splitting. It wasn't so surprising, considering that the unpalatable truth from yesterday evening had been churning in her brain all night. With a busy day ahead, there was no way she was going to function properly, not without paracetamol and some hot, strong coffee.

After a lightning-quick shower, she donned the blue dressing gown and slipped out of her room. It was still very early. The guests would be asleep for hours, she was certain. All was quiet from the guest end of the corridor as she turned down the stairs, even managing to remember to avoid the creaky tread.

In the kitchen, she greeted Major and let him into the garden. It was barely dawn and there'd been a sharp frost. Not unexpected with such a clear night sky like that. She forced away the memory of the romantic moonlit walk in the driveway with Roberto and switched on the espresso maker. Only good strong proper coffee would fix her head; instant just wouldn't hit the spot.

Taking a cup into the office, she switched on the computer. She just had to see those websites again, just to be certain that it wasn't all a product of some feverish dream, brought on by too much good food, wine — and that kiss, of course.

No, it was definitely no fabrication of her mind. There was Roberto's own business website featuring a selection of his photography. She clicked back through the computer's history to find the article on the Di Ferraio family and their noble heritage.

She leaned back in the chair and sighed. Just how much of this did Lauren know? If it came to it, and their love did prove lasting, would it be up to

Beth to explain to her that Luca's cousin didn't think she was good enough?

The coffee and painkillers might have taken the edge off Beth's headache, but they did nothing to ease her indignation and resentment. She trawled through a few more internet pages, and suddenly came across a feature about the Di Ferraio family home.

She hesitated before reading on. It already felt uncomfortably voyeuristic, secretly checking out Roberto.

But surely, she reasoned, just like the Tilney Lodge website, the information was put on there to be seen. And anyway, she was just too curious to resist.

The garden was amazing. The terracing, the narrow waterfalls, the naturalistic planting, so very lush and green — all exactly as Roberto had described, but on so much a grander scale than she'd imagined. She recalled him remarking how he'd love her to see it. It had just been words after all.

An ache pulled at her heart. It wasn't just sadness over her hopeless feelings. She felt incredibly foolish too. In the course of twenty-four hours she'd had to review her impressions of Roberto Di Ferraio at least three times, and this latest version was the least pleasant of all.

'Good morning, Beth. Have you been checking me out!'

His soft, rich voice, so close to her ear, had her jumping from her seat so violently that her head butted his chin. She recoiled and he steadied her, his hands on her arms. 'Whoa, I didn't mean to startle you . . . you okay?'

She shrank away from the pressure of his hands. She wasn't going to go through all that again, her veins tingling and fizzing at his touch. She couldn't meet his eyes, and she couldn't even look at his lips without remembering his kiss. She turned her head away from him completely.

'Yes, I'm fine,' she bridled. 'I just didn't realise anyone else was creeping

153

about this early . . . '

Not only about, but showered and shaved, and dressed in those dark jeans again and another fresh shirt — a pale blue one this time.

Beth tied the belt of the old dressing gown a bit tighter. On her feet were the fluffy panda slippers that Lauren had bought her at Christmas. Once again he'd caught her looking less than her best.

Well so what! She tossed her head. There was definitely no impressing him now anyway. And she wouldn't want him thinking that another member of the family was trying to hook a rich, well-connected husband!

'Luca's still snoring in dreamland! But I woke early and smelt the coffee — ' His smile twinkled. ' — literally! So I thought I'd come down and find some.'

'Do help yourself,' she said, waving in the direction of the kitchen and hoping he'd take the hint. If he thought she was going to serve him, just because he was related to aristocracy or something, he had another think coming!

'Thank you. I will in a moment.'

She was aware of his eyes sliding to the screen on the desk beside her. The shots of the Italian garden were still on display. There was no denying she'd been looking, and nothing for it but to brazen it out. 'I presume you took those pictures,' she said, 'though I gather portraits are more in your line.'

'Yes, I admit most of my — er — snaps do tend to be portraiture . . . '

Beth clamped her teeth together. Yes, why not remind her of all the times she'd belittled his profession. But it wasn't her fault if she hadn't known what he did for his living. But then it wasn't his fault either, argued her reasonable side — and her reasonable side won out.

'Um, I may have come across as a bit dismissive yesterday,' she began stiffly. 'But I had no idea that you were a professional photographer.' Or quite so famous, she added to herself.

'No problem, Beth,' he replied lightly. 'It was a refreshing change, actually. Some people, when they learn what I do, seem to expect me to ask them to be my next model.'

Not just people, she thought. She bet he meant women. Well there was no danger of that with her! She was in no position to put herself in the same category as all those society beauties and celebrities he photographed.

'So what do you think of my mother's garden?' he said, his hand on the back of the chair.

'It's stunning. Absolutely beautiful.' She couldn't deny that, or keep the admiration from her voice. 'And exactly as you described it. In fact,' she added, deciding to call his bluff with a challenge, 'I should love to see it in person . . . '

He confounded her by looking absolutely delighted. 'Then it's a date,' he replied.

Beth was incensed. How could he make that sort of offer when he knew full well that once Luca and Lauren's romance foundered, he'd be off without a backward glance — and no doubt congratulating himself at pulling off a lucky escape?

He really was one cool customer, wasn't he? But then she'd thought that at the very beginning. She wasn't going to let him have everything his own way though. The very least she could do was get him to come out and admit that he thought her sister was a prospective gold-digger.

She steeled her nerves and fixed a smile before turning her face to his. 'That would be lovely. Perhaps I can come over after the wedding. Or *for* the wedding, if Lauren and Luca decide to have the ceremony over there.'

His returning smile dimmed a few watts. 'But I thought we'd agreed . . . '

'I've been thinking it over,' she interrupted, 'and it seems to be me we're being very high-handed about this. Perhaps we're underestimating their feelings. If they say they're in love

157

and want to get married, is it really our place to decide they're too immature to know their own minds? In fact, I'd say it's none of our business . . . Wouldn't you, Roberto?'

His eyes clouded, his lips pursed thoughtfully. 'Hmm, yes, I suppose so . . . although . . . '

She cocked her head enquiringly and waited for him to continue. Would this be where he'd come clean and say that he didn't support the engagement because Lauren wasn't good enough for his family?

But he baffled her again by saying, 'You're right, of course. It's not up to us to decide. We can only guide the people we love.'

'And support them afterwards, of course, if things should — heaven forbid — go disastrously wrong,' she qualified, adding, 'But then again, it might turn out to be very successful.'

'I shouldn't like to see either of them get hurt,' he responded, the quizzical expression still on his face as he continued to study Beth. 'And I gave a promise to Luca's mother that I wouldn't let him do anything rash. My aunt's a widow — Luca's father is dead — and I seem to have been nominated as the family guiding hand of wisdom where my cousin is concerned. He's always been rather popular with the girls — ' He paused with a small rueful smile.

Beth lifted her eyebrows. No doubt it was a problem that ran in his family.

' — and of course he finds all the attention tremendously flattering. But these types of attractions are often fleeting and . . . '

He was waffling! She'd have to be far more direct if she wanted to smoke him out.

'And you wouldn't want him falling into the clutches of the wrong girl!' she snapped, feeling the blood rising in her veins.

He was looking very bewildered now. He took a hesitant step towards her.

'I don't understand, Beth. Yesterday,

I thought we were becoming friends, that we were on the same side. But this morning you're different. Rather angry, I think? Have I done anything to offend you?'

He stood there, gazing at her, looking absolutely stunning, his dark eyes intense and troubled. She felt split in two. Logic told her all the reasons why she had to keep her distance, yet her legs were all for taking that last remaining step and throwing herself into his arms.

She forced herself to stay calm and still, and then to turn away. 'I've got a busy day ahead. Would you excuse me while I get dressed. Then I'll come back down and sort out some breakfast for everyone.'

Beth pulled back the curtains in Lauren's room. Dawn had broken fully now but it was clouding up already and the weather looked doubtful after such a promising, clear start. If there wasn't so much going on, she would have been dressed, outside and busy working while the rain held off.

No wonder she was finding recent events so challenging, her feelings for Roberto so hard to manage. Until his arrival, her life had always been rather predictable and even. She might even say dull, apart from the time she was dealing with Lauren's unpredictable exploits.

Lauren groaned when Beth shook her awake. 'Oh, give over,' she complained drowsily, 'it's the middle of the night. Isn't it?'

'It's half past seven actually, and I need to talk to you.' Beth cleared a pile of clothes from the dressing table stool so she could sit down. 'Exactly how much do you know about Luca's family?'

Sighing and yawning, Lauren sat up and pushed back her thick hair, then blinked at Beth. 'Do you mean do I know how posh they are?'

'Posh! That's one way of putting it. Why on earth didn't you tell me that they're practically Italian nobility? I bet you told your friends. No wonder they were so impressed by Luca.'

Yawning one minute, shrugging the next, Lauren said, 'They might be, but I knew it wouldn't cut any ice with you, Beth.'

'Too right!' Beth exclaimed hotly. 'But I still wish I'd known. I wouldn't feel quite such a fool . . . ' And not only that, she realised, she would have been even more on her guard against falling for Roberto.

'I can't see what the problem is then,' Lauren sighed, sinking back into her pillow. 'You wouldn't have treated them any different if you had known.'

'No, but it would have gone a long way to explain Roberto's big-headedness.'

'Luca isn't at all big-headed though.'

Actually, no — now Beth came to think of it — he wasn't, was he? He did behave just like a normal teenager, albeit an exceptionally good-looking one.

'I mean, I had no idea when I first met him that he was anything more than just a drop-dead gorgeous guy,' added Lauren. 'So at least you can't accuse me of wanting to get my hooks into him for his money!'

Beth winced inwardly. Unfortunately that was precisely what Roberto had come to prevent though, wasn't it?

'Why are you pulling that face?' asked Lauren. 'You don't think that of me, surely?'

'No, of course not! But you're plenty of other things besides ... crazy, impetuous, deceitful. Not to mention grossly unfair to everyone involved. Including me,' she added. 'It's torture having to keep your two engagements a secret. I feel like I'm walking on eggshells all the time, and every time I speak to Roberto I almost go and drop you in it.'

'Oh, please don't Beth. Just give me a couple of days. Ewen's back at the weekend, and then I can put everyone in the picture.'

The weekend felt like a life sentence away. 'Poor Ewen. He's going to be devastated. And then there's Luca.

How do you think he's going to feel knowing you've been engaged to someone else all along?'

Lauren squirmed uncomfortably. 'I should have told him, I know. But it just sort of happened so quickly.'

'You know you may end up with neither of them.'

Lauren looked stricken for a second, but quickly rallied. 'No, it'll be fine. Really. True love always wins out in the end, doesn't it?'

'It might in novels, but not always in real life,' said Beth. Sighing wearily, she got to her feet. 'Are you coming down for breakfast anytime soon? I've got a packed day ahead. I don't know what you and Luca have got planned, but you'd be doing me a favour if you could invite Roberto along . . . '

'Sure, no probs. I'm not sure what we're doing actually, but he can tag along if he wants. Bit of sightseeing, perhaps. I'll come straight down,' she added, throwing back the covers and leaping from bed. 'Just give us a minute

164

to get dressed and do my face — Oh, that reminds me . . . you didn't borrow a lipstick last night, did you? Only one of mine seems to be missing.'

From the door, Beth turned and surveyed the room with wide eyes. 'You're amazing! Your room is a cross between a mammoth jumble sale and the council tip, yet you know when one tiny lipstick has disappeared.'

'That's because it's organised chaos . . . and stop trying to change the subject, Beth! Does Roberto know how honoured he was? You wearing lipstick for a change . . . ?'

Beth opened her mouth to give some retort, but couldn't think of a single thing in her defence. 'Sorry not to have asked before I borrowed it.'

Lauren shook her head, laughing outwardly now. 'Don't be daft. You know you can borrow anything you like.'

Beth headed back to her room to get dressed, wondering if she could borrow some of Lauren's chutzpah. But she guessed it wouldn't suit her.

Pulling on a respectable and clean pair of jeans and a blue and cream sweatshirt, and taking the time to comb and tie her hair back into a neat ponytail, at least she didn't feel quite such a shambolic mess when she returned to the kitchen.

Everyone else was already there. Roberto was making toast, Luca was eating most of it, Major was scrounging for tidbits around their feet, and Lauren was trying to plan the day.

'How about a look round Norwich . . . ?'

'But it's raining,' Luca complained.

Beth glanced at the window and saw he was right. The first few drops were hitting the window pane.

Lauren shrugged. 'So what?'

Luca gave her a puppy dog-eyed look. 'But it messes with my hair . . . '

Beth caught Roberto's lips twitching. She wanted to smile too, and found herself sharing a look of amused complicity with him. That wouldn't do! Lifting her chin, she spun on her heels and began briskly emptying the dish-washer of the evening's crockery. She just wasn't going to allow Roberto to get under her skin like this. Or any deeper than he already was.

Turning sharply to place a pile of clean plates on the worktop, she practically bounced off Roberto's chest. He'd silently crossed the kitchen to offer her a plate of toast. It smelt inviting, but not as tempting as his cologne.

'Thanks,' she shook her head curtly as she stepped aside, 'but I don't usually bother with much more than coffee in the mornings.'

He clicked his tongue and the look he gave her was stern. Yet it still played havoc with her tummy.

'You should start the day with something.'

'You've done nothing but try to feed me up since you've been here,' she said, keeping her voice deliberately light.

'You could do with some feeding up . . .'

She felt his eyes skate up and down her slender figure. No doubt he preferred a more shapely woman.

'... oh, let's go anyway, Luca ...' Lauren's cajoling voice drifted across the kitchen. 'If it's still raining when we get there, we can always hang around the Mall and look round the shops. Or go to the cinema?'

'Yeah, the cinema sounds okay ...'

Beth thought he still didn't sound all that enthusiastic though.

'What about you, Beth ... ?' asked Roberto, leaning casually against the fridge with his arms crossed. 'Have you got plans for today?'

'Oh, lots!' she said emphatically, bustling about the kitchen. 'I've got a couple of marquee enquiries to follow up in Allsham, some supplies to pick up from the garden centre.' And she'd have to fit in some supermarket shopping. The fridge was probably woefully empty, but there was no way she was going to ask him to move away so she could check. 'I expect you'll be going

168

along to Norwich with Lauren and Luca, won't you?' He could try and put a spoke in the wheels of the romance at the same time.

'To the cinema? You're joking! Luca's only into aliens and CGI, and they both bore me stiff. Actually I've a couple of long-standing business invitations in London. I may as well take them up seeing as I'm over here.'

'London?' Beth frowned, her mind twirling with the practicalities. She certainly didn't have time to chauffeur him. Not that she had the slightest desire to do so. And she doubted if the Toyota would make such long trips on two days running without blowing a gasket or something. He'd have to go by rail.

She started opening and closing kitchen drawers. 'I'm sure we've got a timetable somewhere. There's an occasional train that runs from Allsham, but your best bet would be to catch one from Norwich station. There's an express that goes straight to Liverpool

Street, if that's any good . . . ?' She guessed the sort of invitations Roberto received were likely to be located in the West End. 'You could catch a cab across town from there though.'

'Transport's all in hand. I booked a hire car from the garage in Allsham yesterday.'

She stared at him in surprise. He'd never said. But then again, why should he?

He straightened up, pushed back his right cuff to look at his watch. 'As you're going in yourself, Beth, perhaps you wouldn't mind giving me a lift to the garage. If it's not too much trouble?'

8

If he'd gone so far as to arrange a hire car to be delivered to the little garage in Allsham, then surely he could have had it brought up to the Lodge, she speculated, as the Toyota splashed through the wet country lanes.

Once again, Roberto was peering out at the passing scenery. He'd changed after breakfast, and was back in his stunning blue-black suit. She was desperately curious about his long-standing London appointments. What were they? Beautiful, wealthy society women who wanted to commission Roberto to take their portrait?

No camera bag with him, she noticed, so he wouldn't be taking any pictures today. So what then? Just cosy little discussions in luxury London apartments . . . ?

At the sound of a ringtone, he

suddenly produced an ultra-slender, shiny black phone from his pocket. 'Ah, this may be a call I've been expecting. Would you excuse me?'

She nodded, again struck by his polite manners. Her own were nowhere near as polished, as was proved by her eagerly listening in to the conversation.

'Hello? . . . *Hey, Leola, ciao! . . . Sto bene, grazie; e tu? . . .* '

Well, she would have listened in, if it hadn't continued to be in Italian.

Apart from gathering he was talking to a woman called Leola, she didn't have a clue what he was saying. Except that it sounded light-hearted yet rather intimate at the same time. But Leola might not be a girlfriend at all, Beth told herself to ease the streak of jealousy that shot through her. Perhaps she was reading too much into the accent. It was such a beautiful sounding language. For a second she allowed his voice to wash over her, to imagine she was on the receiving end of his Roman charm.

' . . . *ci vediamo, Leola. Tra poco. Si.*'

The ending of the conversation brought Beth to with a sigh.

His head turned immediately.

'It's a pity you have commitments of your own today, Beth. I was going to ask you to join me.'

Her heart leapt before she could stop it.

'It's impossible,' she replied quickly, before temptation got the better of her. Anyway, he had his appointments to make. He wouldn't want her tagging along. She wouldn't want to tag along anyway. 'I've made my arrangements. People are expecting me. I can't run a successful business by letting down prospective customers.'

'My appointments are business too,' he replied, 'but neither should take very long to complete. I was going to suggest lunch at a little restaurant I know — oh,' he broke off, grimacing slightly, 'sorry, I'm pushing you at food again!'

She murmured non-commitally. Food

was the last thing on her mind. On the one hand — if circumstances were normal — she would have loved to spend the day with him. But circumstances were far from normal. She felt stressed out, not only for fear of dropping a clanger over Lauren's secret, but also because her attraction to Roberto was in danger of turning her into a nervous wreck.

She shook her head as she conversed silently with herself. Knowing he didn't consider her step-sister good enough for his family, yet still she was drawn to this man. She couldn't understand that at all. It didn't say very much for her own strength of character, did it?

Oh, get a grip, Beth, she told herself sharply, changing down a gear as they passed the Allsham town sign and entered the thirty-mile-an-hour zone. What she needed to do was to flush Roberto into the open. Then he could drop the charm act. As soon as she saw the real Roberto, hopefully it would put her off him for good.

'I'm quite surprised you're not sticking close to Luca and Lauren today,' she said. 'The Norwich shopping-cum-cinema expedition may only be a ruse. Perhaps they're sneaking off to the registrar's office!'

Her words didn't cause a ripple in his calm exterior. 'I doubt it.' He shook his head. 'Even Luca wouldn't dare do that. When someone in our family gets married, it's a big deal. The full works.'

'That's what Lauren's always wanted, the dream white wedding,' she murmured.

There! Roberto reacted to that. But of course, Beth was thinking of Lauren's wedding to Ewen. That was at the core of the problem, wasn't it? If only she hadn't promised to keep Lauren's secret. She sighed again.

'What about you, Beth?'

'Me? Well, it's up to her what sort of wedding she has, isn't it,' she replied cautiously. And to which fiancé, she added silently. 'Lauren will do exactly what she wants at the end of the day. As long as she's in love with her groom . . . ' She might as well get that rubbed in.

'No, I meant what sort of wedding do you dream of?'

'Oh, I see . . . Me?' What on earth did that have to do with anything? She sneaked a sideways glance. He was staring at her — expectantly.

She'd never really envisaged any sort of wedding at all for herself. Perhaps if she'd ever been in love before, her thoughts might have turned to dresses, churches and flowers. Definitely the right sort of flowers.

'I think it should be a joint decision between the couple concerned,' she said, 'But as long as they're in love, then everything else is detail.'

'Ah!' he exclaimed. 'My sentiment exactly. But that's our worry, isn't it, that this isn't love, but will turn out to be a passing infatuation?'

When she didn't comment, he gave a small sound of irritation. 'I just feel that it's my duty to ensure they don't make a mistake the pair of them will live to regret. I've promised Luca's mother I'd keep an eye on him. She's not been in good health, and she worries about him. Please, Beth, try and see this from my viewpoint?'

Beth remained silent, wrestling with guilt over having to force the issue and anger because he still wasn't coming close to admitting the truth. On top of that was the realisation that both of them were bound by promises that didn't sit easily.

'Look, Beth, if I thought Luca and Lauren were a real love match, then of course I'd be behind them.'

'But you don't think Lauren is right for Luca, do you?' she replied tightly.

'Neither do you. Or so you told me last night. But this morning, for some unfathomable reason, you've changed your mind. Something has happened overnight and unless you tell me what, how can I put things right between us . . . ?'

Her heart weighed heavily with the

knowledge that things could never be right between them.

Beth pulled up outside the garage forecourt and turned to look at him. Instantly his hand reached for hers. His touch sent a series of electric shocks rippling across her skin. His eyes raked her face.

But however much his gaze and his touch affected her, distracted her, she needed to see his reaction.

She took a deep breath. 'I don't think you can put things right. Even if you changed your mind, or admitted you were in the wrong, it doesn't change the fact that you think Lauren's not good enough to marry into your family.'

His eyes widened and he almost laughed. 'You're joking! No, my God, you're not joking. Where on earth did you get that idea from — ?' He broke off, his eyes gleaming. 'No, don't tell me. I think I know . . . It's not just my home and my career you've been checking up on, but my background too!'

She blushed violently. 'Have I got it so very wrong then?' she challenged, tugging her hand away from his, furious that he seemed to be, first, humouring her, then dismissing her natural indignation so lightly. 'You and Luca aren't descended from Italian nobility then?'

He lifted his chin. Fire flashed in his eyes. Suddenly he was every inch an aristocrat. 'I'm not ashamed of my heritage or my family background, but it hasn't the slightest bearing on whether Luca and Lauren have a future together. And as for your sister not being good enough — ' He tailed off, apparently struggling to find the right words. 'Frankly, I've no idea how you arrived at that ridiculous conclusion. And I'm appalled to learn that you should think that of me.'

He twisted away from her.

Beth swallowed hard. He'd turned it around so now she was on the back foot. She'd offended him terribly, she could see that. But was it also unjustly? Could she have got it wrong? A small voice in her ear was telling her she might have jumped to the wrong conclusion. His denial had certainly come across as sincere, though while she was feeling so confused it was difficult to trust her own judgement. All she knew for definite was that her stomach had just dropped several stories lower.

'Roberto — ?' she began, her voice almost a whisper. 'I didn't — '

A shadow looming up at the driver's side window signalled the arrival of someone from the garage's office.

'I think they're waiting to hand over your hire car,' she said dully.

Roberto sprang out of the van without a word or a glance for her. He closed the door softly. It gave her a small splinter of hope. If he was angry, surely he would have slammed it? But so soft was his touch that the door hadn't caught, and she had to lean across to pull it to.

She stayed in that position, watching Roberto stride across the forecourt, signing paperwork on the mechanic's clipboard as he did so. Accepting the keys and nodding at the man, he folded himself into the silver Mercedes and roared away.

Beth cajoled the Toyota into gear and stuttered along the road, feeling like it was the end of the world.

* * *

'This is the spot where we thought the marquee might go . . . ' The family showed Beth through to their back garden, and she surveyed the site for evenness of ground and any low-branched overhanging trees.

'No, I think it would be fine here. It's a lovely location. When is your daughter's wedding?'

'The first Saturday in September,' grimaced the bride's mother. 'It sounds ages away, but it's rushing up on us far too fast.'

Beth nodded sympathetically. Didn't she just know all about it. It was supposed to be less than three months to Lauren's wedding to Ewen — although she couldn't see that happening now. She ought to make a start on cancelling everything as soon as possible. Unless crazy Lauren was determined to go ahead with it — but with one key change. A different groom.

Forcing her thoughts back to the job in hand, after discussing the terms and making sure the family were happy with everything, she entered the date in her diary.

Usually she would have been delighted with the booking, but today everything was tarnished by her inner turmoil. She got back in the Toyota and drove across town to her next appointment, grateful to be busy at least.

She was finished before lunch, and decided to fit in a supermarket shop before heading back to the Lodge. Lauren's Mini was missing, so Beth concluded she must have gone into

Norwich with Luca after all. Roberto would be in London by now. She pushed away an unbidden image of him wining and dining some Italian beauty, the Leola of the phone conversation probably. After learning Beth's opinion of him, he'd be congratulating himself that he hadn't lumbered himself with her for the day after all.

Juggling several carrier bags, Beth let herself in through the side door to the silent kitchen. After the high octane roller coaster of the last twenty-four hours, it was a respite to have the place all to herself. Except for Major, of course. He came up, wagging his tail and smiling in his usual uncomplicated way, before thrusting his nose into the supermarket carriers.

'Come on then!' she relented. 'Let's see if there's anything in here for you . . .'

After she'd taken everything out of the bags and stood it on the side, she stood looking at it for a second or two, wondering why it seemed different.

None of the usual processed and convenience foods, she'd gone for speciality bread and cooked meats, some Italian cheese, lots of fresh fruit and vegetables, and a jar of olives! Had Roberto really had such an impact on her that he'd managed to change her shopping habits!

Or was she — despite her lofty intentions and misplaced accusations — simply trying to impress him after all? Talk about whistling in the wind!

'Oh, Major!' she sighed, fondling his ears. 'How I am going to deal with this?' He rested his muzzle on her knees and studied her with his faithful eyes.

As delicious as the bread and cheese was, Beth found it turned to cotton wool in her mouth. She kept getting flashbacks of Roberto stalking away from the van, his body language so cold and controlled.

Had she jumped to completely the wrong idea about his motivations? Bound by the promise to his aunt, did he really only have Luca's emotional welfare at heart? If so, she'd made the most monumental mistake, and doubted if he'd ever forgive the insult.

She couldn't sit still and keep going over and over the same ground without sending herself mad. Keeping busy was the answer. Jumping up, she took a glossy red apple and a glass of water into the office, and noted down the information for the two marquee booking dates. The diary was looking very full from early summer, stretching right into the autumn. As well as garden tours, there was a series of weekend courses running over the holiday months. And a television company was coming to film for a whole week at the end of September too. None of these enterprises would make her rich, but they did mean she could hang on to her home, the house that her parents had loved. Staying on at the Lodge had been far from a certainty after her father had died and she'd learned the precariousness of their financial situation. She could be proud of how she'd managed to grasp the challenge and develop ways of bringing in income.

When a thin slant of pale sunlight fell through the window, she decided to take advantage and get some outside work done while there was a break in the weather.

'You coming too, Major?' she said, brushing his head with her fingertips as she passed. 'No?'

Leaving the door ajar in case he wanted to follow her out in his own time, she collected tools from the shed and was soon absorbed by a problem in the garden.

Water, she noticed, was pooling in an area where it shouldn't be, which could only mean one of the overflow channels leading from the lake was blocked. It was messy, arduous work, digging out the soil, but eventually she located and repositioned the sunken drain.

By the time she'd finished, it was late, coming on to rain again, and she was absolutely filthy and caked in mud from head to foot. But it was satisfying to know she'd forestalled the potential problem of a completely flooded garden. Squelching up to the side door and dragging off her boots on the step, she was more than ready for a hot drink and something to eat.

She'd have to start thinking about putting together something for supper. What time would everyone else be back? Perhaps Roberto would stay down in London overnight? Her heart took a sudden nosedive. She hoped not. She wanted to explain — or as much as she could — and to apologise for what she'd said that morning.

But he'd have the courtesy to let her know if wasn't coming back tonight, wouldn't he? She checked the phones. There'd been no messages left on her mobile, and nothing on the answerphone either.

'No news is good news, Major . . . ' she suggested with more optimism than she felt. 'Major?' She glanced around the kitchen. No dog, and his basket was empty too. It was unusual for him not to stick close by. Pushing away a sense of unease, she went to the door. A combination of dusk and an impending downpour was making the light even murkier.

She called out his name several times. He'd come trotting in any minute. Leaving the door open, she went to fill the kettle. It had hardly begun to sing before she was at the door again, calling his name.

'Major! Teatime!' Food, that would bring him in.

But it didn't. She tried to remember when she'd last seen him. She'd been engrossed in the drainage work most of the afternoon. At one point he'd been snuffling along the edge of the lake, but that must have been over an hour ago.

She switched the kettle off. Collecting a torch, she jammed her feet back into wet boots and ran out into the garden. Calling and searching the grounds proved fruitless.

Tears started to drip down her face and merge with the rain. All the while she'd been searching she'd been fighting a rising sense of panic. Some inner sense told her something was very wrong.

If he wasn't in the garden he must have wandered further afield. Running out of the gates, Beth began blaming herself for not noticing his absence earlier. Searching in the daylight she might have stood a chance. In the darkness, and with the heavy rain now falling, it was all but impossible.

She ran the torch beam over the grass verges, but the beam it gave was narrow and inadequate. Where might he have gone?

As she searched the hedgerows that bordered the lane, an occasional vehicle whizzed past, sending up spray, and causing Beth to press herself into the hedge for safety. What if he'd been run over? No, she told herself, she'd have heard the commotion. Wouldn't she?

Pushing away ghastly images of calamitous scenes, she methodically searched both sides of the road, periodically calling out Major's name.

And finally she was rewarded with an answering low bark.

'Major!' Thank goodness. He was here somewhere, and he was alive.

She eventually tracked him down in one of the ditches that ran parallel with the hedgerow. She slithered down the steep sides, flashing the beam of light from left to right until it fell on her dog.

He was a bedraggled sight, standing up in about a half a metre of water, but soaked all over.

'Oh, Major, what on earth have you done?' she wailed, thrusting the torch in her pocket so she could take his head in both hands. His tail flickered miserably. 'Are you hurt? Can you get out?'

She felt for his collar and urged him forward. He made to move, but yelped. 'Sorry, boy.' She winced for him.

Using the torch again, she noticed the ditch water had a pinkish tinge to it. Blood! Or just a trick of the dim light? Had he broken something? How serious was it? She was going to have to get him out of there somehow.

She tried to lift him, but he was wet and heavy, and each time she moved him he whimpered in pain.

'It's all right, boy. Don't worry,' she soothed, forcing her voice to sound calm for his sake, while inwardly she was frantic.

She couldn't do this alone, she had to get help.

Her phone! It wasn't in any of her pockets. Had she dropped it in the water while she was trying to lift him, or had she left it in the kitchen? The picture slotted into her head of it laying on the kitchen worktop.

Stupid, stupid, stupid! she raged inwardly.

'I'm going to have to leave you to get help,' she told him. How long would it take to climb out, and run to the Lodge and back? It would seem like an eternity to Major. She didn't even know who she would ring for help.

Kissing the dog's head, she turned the torch beam away so she didn't have to see his pained and pleading eyes as she left him.

It took several attempts to clamber up the sheer side of the ditch.

Her feet kept slipping back down through the sticky clay soil, but eventually she managed to grab a root and with a bit of momentum, haul up herself up and over.

And right into the path of a pair of oncoming headlamps.

9

How the car managed to avoid her, she would never know.

With a squeal of brakes, the wheels locked and the vehicle skidded and spun across the wet road and slewed to a halt against the opposite bank. If something had been coming the other way . . . she couldn't bear to think what the consequences might have been.

Gasping, she fell back against the hedgerow, while in apparent slow motion the driver's door opened and a man in a dark suit scrambled out. Could it possibly be . . . ?

'Roberto?' she whispered. It felt like a miracle.

'Beth!' He rushed over and held her up by the arms. 'Are you all right? I could have killed you! What on earth are you doing out here in this?'

She gazed up at him, only half seeing

him in the light from the headlamps. Raindrops were pouring down her face — raindrops and tears.

'It's . . . Major . . . ' she sobbed, the shock making her barely able to string any words together. 'He's . . . in the ditch . . . something's wrong with him . . . I can't lift him out. Got to ring someone . . . my phone . . . up at the Lodge . . . '

'Where, Beth?' His firm hands rocked her arms. 'Where is he exactly?'

She turned, her head indicating the spot.

'Let me try.' His hands dropped away and she almost sank to the ground. 'Can you move the car, Beth,' he called, already slithering half-way down into the ditch. 'It might cause an accident where it is.'

Pausing only to hand down the torch, she got into the Mercedes. The controls were a mystery. But he'd left the keys in the ignition. Somehow she managed to turn the car around and park it with its nose just inside the Lodge's driveway.

Then she stumbled back along the verge. It was almost pitch black now and the rain was falling in torrents. 'Roberto? Where are you? Have you found him?'

'Here.' The torch shone up, blinding her momentarily. 'He's caught up on something. It feels like wire.'

She slithered down and landed with a splash in the water. It was deeper now. More rainwater was draining off from the saturated fields.

'Here, hold the torch . . . ' he said. 'Try and keep it steady.'

That was easier said than done. Her hands were shaking through cold and shock. But Roberto was calm, soothing Major with soft words, while methodically working away with his hands under the water. There was definitely blood in the water. They had to get him out of there and to a vet as soon as possible.

'It's curled round his back legs mainly . . . but nearly there. Right, that's all of it, I think.' He lifted from the water a twisted length of rusty barbed wire.

'It's lethal,' she gasped. 'Poor Major.'

Roberto's hands were running with pink-tinged water. Had he been cut too?

'Now all we've got to do is lift him out,' he said.

She never knew how they managed to do it. Major was shivering and whimpering as Roberto took the bulk of his weight and hoisted him up. Beth could do little more than steady the dog's front end and help keep the pair of them from overbalancing. Somehow they inched up the side of the ditch and out onto to the grass verge. Blood was pouring from one of Major's back legs. Roberto was soaked through, his suit flattened to his body, his hair to his skull. The rain was still lashing down.

'He'll be okay, Beth,' he said, 'But we need to get him checked by a vet.'

She knew he was keeping deliberately calm for her benefit.

'We can take him straight there?'

She nodded. 'The vet's surgery is in Allsham.' It would be quicker than going back to the Lodge, ringing and waiting for the duty vet to come out.

Beth, wielding the torch, led the way back along the verge to the Mercedes. Roberto, carrying Major, followed, and laid him tenderly on the back seat.

'The car . . . We're all filthy . . . ' she began.

'Do you really think that matters,' he said curtly. 'Will you sit in beside him and keep him as still as possible . . . ' Once she was inside, he closed the door and dashed round to the driver's side.

'I've no idea how long he was stuck there,' she chided herself aloud, stroking Major's head in her lap. 'I should have noticed earlier that he'd wandered off.'

'No point blaming yourself, Beth,' said Roberto, deftly turning the car around and pulling out onto the main road. 'You found him, that's the main thing.'

She nodded. She wouldn't have given

up looking until she had found him. But what if Roberto hadn't turned up when he did . . . ? 'I'd never have got him out if you hadn't come along.'

'Then I'm doubly relieved.'

'Doubly?'

'For managing to help get him out. And for not running over you before you could tell me what was wrong! You scared the life out me when you appeared in the road like that.' He patted his heart.

'I'm really sorry, Roberto,' she said in a tiny voice.

'No need to sound so penitent,' he said. 'It was only my poor attempt at trying to cheer you up.'

She glanced up and met his concerned eyes briefly in the rear view mirror. Did he realise, she wondered, that her apology was for far more than nearly frightening him to death.

'How does he seem now?'

'I'm not sure.' She wiped the water away from Major's eyes, and lifted his head so his muzzle rested on her knees.

His body continued to tremble as she ran her hands down his back. The cuts on his back legs were still oozing blood, but at least it wasn't pouring out.

'Soon be there.' Roberto drove fast, faster than she would have dared on wet and unfamiliar roads in an unfamiliar car, the wipers going at full pelt — and yet she felt perfectly safe with him at the wheel. He slowed down when they reached the outskirts of town, and Beth directed him through the streets to the surgery.

She suddenly wondered what time it was. Would the surgery still be open?

A petite figure in a full-length wax waterproof coat was just locking up the main door when they arrived in the floodlit car park. 'Oh, thank goodness,' she breathed, 'we're not too late. And that's Fleur, our regular vet.'

Roberto carried Major inside and onto the examination table. Beth related what she thought had happened.

'Major, I'm surprised at you,' Fleur

admonished gently, as she gave him a comprehensive examination. 'Getting into mischief at your age. I thought you'd have known better by now!'

'Has he injured himself very seriously?' Beth asked anxiously. Despite the water still dripping from her hair and clinging to her face, her eyes felt red hot and boiled dry. 'All that blood — ?'

Roberto's arm curled round her protectively, and she instinctively leaned into his body. He looked almost as anxious as she felt. Anxious and very, very wet and filthy dirty, she realised. And his hands had been torn to shreds on the wire too. She looked up from them to him, and winced on his behalf.

'Well, no real harm done,' Fleur finally pronounced with a smile, after lowering her stethoscope. 'There are some nasty cuts to his paws. He's ripped off a toenail, which is where most of the blood was coming from. He's in a bit of shock, very cold and sorry for himself. But he should be as right as rain in a day or two. I'll just get a couple of injections into him, an antibiotic and one for the pain, if you can keep him steady on the table for a second . . . ' Fleur disappeared through a door into the dispensary.

Beth stood by Major's head, silent tears of relief pouring down her face. She dropped a kiss on the dog's skull.

Roberto loomed up beside her. His hand reached out and thumbed the moisture away from under her eyes. Beth's breath caught in her throat. She couldn't begin to think what a sight she must be.

'Don't cry, Beth. You're dripping all over the nice vet's clean floor!'

She glanced at him, feeling shy. 'Well you can talk!'

'Thanks!' Glancing down at his clothes, he grinned ruefully. 'Yes, I think I can safely say this suit will never be quite the same again!'

'Oh dear!' Beth bit her lip. That was her fault. But he still looked fantastic in it, though, didn't he?

Fleur came back in with an armful of treatments. 'I'll clean the worst of the wounds and put a bandage on the paw with the cut pad. You'll need to keep that dry.' She passed some antiseptic cream, cotton wool and plasters to Beth. 'And these are for the human injuries!'

While Fleur treated a very patient and well-behaved Major, Roberto washed his hands in the little basin in the corner of the surgery. Then Beth proceeded to gently dab the cuts and scrapes clean, smooth on the cream and apply the plasters. A mixture of overwrought emotions and the hand to hand contact made her all fingers and thumbs.

'I wouldn't make a very good nurse,' she mumbled.

'Oh, I don't know,' he replied, 'they're feeling better already.' Which she thought was incredibly courteous of him, considering the circumstances.

From the surgery's reception area, watching Roberto tenderly carrying Major back to the car, Fleur gently squeezed Beth's arm. 'What an absolutely gorgeous man! Where on earth did you find him?'

'It's a long story,' sighed Beth.

'And one that's not over yet, I think!' Fleur replied with a knowing expression.

Roberto drove back to the Lodge at a more sedate pace. Finally the rain had eased to a steady drizzle.

'You're shaking.' He glanced over his shoulder into the back seat, where again Beth was sitting with Major propped up against her. 'You'd better have a large brandy and a hot bath as soon as we get home . . . '

Home? Her heart lurched at the way he said it. For a second it was heaven to pretend the Lodge was their home together . . .

'You don't want to end up catching the flu.'

She attempted a grin through chattering teeth. If only he knew the delirium had already started!

He pressed a few buttons on the

dashboard. 'There, I've put the heater on full blast.'

'I'll be fine. You're just as soaked as I am. And I am worried about your suit . . . '

'It doesn't matter, Beth. Really. Suits can be replaced. But dogs cannot. Or people . . . certain people . . . '

His voice had become so faint she wasn't entirely sure she heard that last bit correctly.

'I'm glad it didn't happen before you went to London. Did your meetings go okay?' She hadn't intended on being so nosey, but there, she'd asked it now.

He nodded. 'Yes, they did. Both galleries are interested in running exhibitions of my photographs.'

'Oh, galleries!' Relief surged through her and she smiled at him in the rear view mirror.

He caught her eyes and grinned back, an inquisitive tilt to his eyebrows.

'I thought perhaps you had — um — appointments with private clients . . . ' Feeling her cheeks flaming, her voice tailed off. She dropped her head to check on Major.

'Is he okay?'

'Yes, he's seems fine. Sleepy. But Fleur said he would be after the sedative she gave him kicked him.'

Roberto nodded. 'Along with the course of antibiotics, rest and quiet will be the best medicine.'

'Hmm.' For Major, yes. But not for her. She needed to clear the air with Roberto. Or as much as was possible without breaking her word to Lauren.

Rehearsing an apology in her head, she cleared her throat, but before she could speak, Roberto suddenly said, 'Weren't you supposed to be at choir practice this evening?'

'Oh, no! I forgot all about that. What on earth's the time?'

Roberto glanced at the dashboard clock. 'Seven-fifteen.'

'Is that all?' It was too late for the practice, but it felt later than that somehow. After all the drama, and now cocooned in warm luxury it could have been the middle of the night. Romantic music was coming softly from the door speakers, a man singing something in Italian. It could only be a love song.

'Not too loud for Major, is it?'

'No, it's lovely,' she murmured.

'Do you like it? He's one of my favourite artists. I picked up a CD of his in town.'

'What's he singing about?' she asked wistfully.

'Hmm, it's a bit of a long story. But he's asking his girl to forgive him. We don't know if she does.'

'I think she should. I would, if he was singing to me like that. Which reminds me . . . I'll have to ring Kevin and apologise when I get back.'

Roberto's reflected eyes twinkled at her. 'You don't sound as sorry as you should be!'

That was true enough. Though she hated letting anyone down without an explanation, it was a relief not to have to field enquiries about Lauren's impending wedding to Ewen, especially if Roberto had accompanied her as he'd threatened.

'That's why I came back early, so I could go with you to the church. See the famous rood screen.' He shrugged. 'Ah, well, another time, perhaps.'

She suddenly felt deflated. There wouldn't be another time. Despite her brief support for Lauren and Luca's engagement, it was bound to fizzle out sooner or later, and there'd be no reason for Roberto to come back.

It was a heart-breaking thought. She couldn't bear the idea of him taking away a memory of her accusation from this morning without at least trying to explain some of it.

'Roberto,' she began, 'about what I said — '

'Hmm? Oh, a welcoming committee — ' Roberto had slowed to take the turning into the Lodge gates. He stopped the car and the window slid down. Luca's curious face appeared, only to be quickly pushed aside by Lauren's anxious one.

'Roberto, is Beth with you? Oh, there you are!' she exclaimed, spotting Beth in the back. 'I've been so worried — ' Already wide-eyed at their mud-splattered appearance, she caught sight of Major and gave a little shriek. 'Oh, my gosh! Is he all right? What happened?' She opened the back door and scrambled in.

'He had a bit of a mishap, but we managed to catch Fleur at the surgery and he's going to be fine.'

Luca darted round to the front passenger seat, and Roberto drove on up to the Lodge.

'I told Lauren there would be nothing to worry about,' said Luca, as the trio followed Roberto, who was carrying Major from the car through to his basket in the kitchen. 'But she just went into panic overload.'

'Is it any wonder!' Lauren turned on him. 'The house in darkness. No Major . . . ' She turned back to Beth. 'You apparently missing. But your van still parked round the side. I tried ringing you . . . '

'Then found your phone on the kitchen table,' added Luca, rolling his eyes.

'Sorry, guys,' murmured Beth, as she and Lauren fussed round Major.

Lauren brought across the water bowl, and the dog had a few laps before sinking back heavily into his blanket.

Beth quickly related what had happened. Lauren began gently rubbing the dog's fur dry with a towel.

'Your dog will be okay now?' said Luca, leaning his back against a worktop.

'I hope so. Thank goodness your cousin came along.' She threw a shy glance at Roberto, who was making a large pot of tea.

Lauren giggled. 'At one point, I even wondered if Roberto had kidnapped you, Beth!'

Roberto turned to reveal such an affronted expression, that everyone laughed. Beth looked away. She wouldn't need kidnapping to go away with Roberto; she'd happily volunteer!

Embarrassed and annoyed by her untrustworthy emotions, she stood up briskly. 'I'm going up to get cleaned up and changed.'

'Take this with you then,' said Roberto, handing her a mug of hot tea, along with a concerned look. 'You're still shivering. Do you have any whisky to put in it?'

'In the dining room sideboard,' she pointed.

'Shall we start on dinner?' Lauren called after them.

Beth turned. Luca was already rootling in the fridge. It was a good job she had stocked up earlier.

'Good idea,' Roberto chipped in before Beth could answer.

Earlier, she'd been wondering what to do this evening, whether to book a restaurant or even go to the pub in Shallingham. But that was a non-starter in case they bumped into anyone who mentioned Ewen. And now, of course, she didn't want to leave Major by himself.

'Would you mind taking pot luck?' she asked Roberto, as they climbed the stairs.

'No, of course not.' He paused, then added, 'Is Lauren a good cook?'

'Brilliant — if you like burnt beans on burnt toast! But Luca's there to help her.'

'Luca! He struggles with a tin opener! But no matter. I'm so ravenous I'll eat whatever they put in front of me.'

'What about that little restaurant in London? Weren't you planning on having your lunch there?'

They'd stopped at the top of the stairs. Standing very close, he looked down at her. 'Only if you'd have been able to come with me. Alone, I decided not to bother.'

'Couldn't you have had lunch with one of your business appointments?'

'Leola, you mean?' His expression showed amusement. 'She had a previous engagement.'

'Leola?' she said innocently, as if she

couldn't quite place the name. But there was no fooling Roberto. He could see straight through her, as usual.

Why did he have to look at her like that? As if she was the most important, precious thing in his life. She couldn't bear it.

He reached out for her. She twisted aside, preparing to turn away, but misjudged his intention. His hand cupped her chin and, with the gentlest of touches, lifted her head so she was forced to meet his eyes.

'There, that's better,' he murmured, taking another half step closer. 'Why do you shy away from looking at me all the time, Beth? Am I so very terrible to look at!'

She smiled, even though she was aching inside. If only he knew. If he was an inanimate object of beauty — a painting or a statue — she could happily feast her eyes on him until the end of her days. All in a purely objective way. Because it wouldn't ignite sparklers in her stomach, send fireworks zipping through her veins, make her heart beat like a drum, or turn her knees and brain to cotton wool.

'I — I — ' she stuttered. He loomed up even closer. She steeled herself to withstand his kiss. Instead, his lips brushed the top of her still damp hair. And she felt utterly cheated.

10

'This looks great,' remarked Beth, gazing appreciatively over the food spread out over the kitchen table. She felt better for a hot shower and a change into dry clothes, even if they were only simple clean jeans and tunic top.

'I'm impressed!' she added, bending down to check on Major, who was thankfully resting peacefully in his basket without any signs of distress. She was glad they were eating in the kitchen though, just so she could keep an eye on him.

'You needn't look quite so surprised,' Lauren said indignantly, waving a set of salad servers. 'I'm not that clueless at getting a meal together.'

'No?' retorted Beth. 'You've kept very quiet about it all these years then!'

'Actually, I prepared most of this,'

Luca interjected, with a superior air.

'It's only a bit of salad so I shouldn't think Jamie Oliver's quaking in his trainers!' said Roberto. He strode across the room, glancing at the table. He'd changed back into jeans, too, and his blue checked shirt, now with the sleeves rolled up. Beth noted his hair was still wet where it curled behind his ears, this time from the shower though, rather than the torrential rain.

Luca's lip dropped petulantly. Beth caught a look of exasperation on Lauren's face. Now she thought about it, there'd been tension between the pair of them earlier, but they'd all been too busy with Major to take much notice. She watched Luca take a seat at one end of the table, and Lauren deliberately go to the other end. It left two seats along one side for her and Roberto. She guessed he'd picked up on the strained atmosphere because of the triumphant expression that crossed his face as he sat down beside her.

Beth pressed her lips together. If the gloss was wearing off Lauren and Luca's romance, then it would confirm her initial misgivings. And much better they discover their mistake now rather than rush into some impulsive wedding. She felt nothing but relief over that.

But what stung was the thought of Roberto's satisfaction if — or, increasingly more likely, when — the engagement was called off. His job here would be over and he could go back home and get on with his life.

The realisation that her life would never be the same again after he'd gone felt like all the life draining from her blood. She couldn't even summon the energy to feel anger that she'd allowed herself to fall under his spell.

While Beth stared down and twiddled listlessly with the salad on her plate, Roberto quizzed Luca about his trip to Norwich.

'It was of a bit of a drag . . . trailing round after Lauren while she tried on clothes.'

'Thanks very much!' muttered Lauren.

Despite herself Beth smiled inwardly, even though it didn't translate to her face. She thought of many the Saturday afternoon Ewen had endured while Lauren was on a fashion shopping fix. But then he'd always suffered whatever Lauren threw at him in silence . . . because he loved her. What must it be like to be adored like that? And Lauren was on the brink of throwing it all away. The girl really was a fool.

'You don't know how spoilt you've been!' she said suddenly.

She must have spoken more sharply than she'd intended, because everyone's head spun to her.

Lauren, turning pink, gulped hard. 'Actually, I'm beginning to realise it.' Her eyes met Beth's uncomfortably before glancing down the table at Luca.

Beth caught her breath, certain that Lauren was finally about to say something.

But if she was, it was cut short by the telephone ringing in the office.

'The answerphone will kick in,' said Beth. But Roberto was already getting to his feet. She looked at him in surprise.

'Do you mind if I answer it? I'm expecting a call back. I gave this number to both the galleries today, in case they couldn't reach me on the mobile.'

'Of course.' She nodded.

' — Oh! Oh, hello! Yes, of course, I do . . . '

Beth strained to hear the one-sided conversation. Roberto's surprised response made her think that it wasn't Leola, or any other caller he'd been expecting.

'No, I'm sorry, we both are. We intended to call you, but it went right out of our minds . . . '

Kevin! Beth pushed back her chair. They'd spoken about calling him to apologise for her non-appearance at choir practice and then it had slipped her mind again.

' . . . a bit of a situation with Beth's dog,' Roberto was saying. 'No, he's fine now, thank you. Yes, I'll tell her . . . '

She'd reached the office doorway. Still listening, he pointed to the phone and mouthed, 'The vicar. Do you want to speak with him?'

Beth shook her head. Roberto had apologised. She didn't really want to relive the dramatic rescue experience again if she could help it. 'Tell him, I promise to be there at the next one,' she whispered.

But Roberto was concentrating. 'Sorry, Kevin . . . Oh? I don't think I quite understand . . . ?'

Beth watched Roberto's face change as he listened, his forehead creasing in a quizzical frown. What on earth was Kevin saying?

'I see. Okay. Yes, I'll pass that message on to Lauren,' he finally said.

'What message?' Lauren called through, as soon as Roberto replaced the receiver. Beth deduced the kitchen conversation had been non-existent if Lauren had been able to hear what was being said in the office.

Beth looked up questioningly at Roberto, but he merely walked towards her in the doorway, leaving her no choice but to turn around and go back to the table.

Roberto resumed his place beside Beth before answering Lauren's question.

'Kevin said to remind you both about your pre-marriage meeting at the vicarage this weekend. Saturday at noon. I think he was rather confused though. He didn't mention Luca's name at all . . . '

Lauren filled the pause. 'No, he said Ewen, didn't he? Me and Ewen.'

Roberto nodded.

Suddenly a pin dropping in the room would have sounded like cannon fire. Sitting so close beside him, yet Beth couldn't even hear Roberto breathing.

'Huh?' Luca, with his fork halfway between plate and mouth, asked, 'Who? Who's Ewen?'

Lauren's voice, when it came, was quiet, with the slightest trace of defiance. 'He's my fiancé, Ewen Walkis. I was already engaged to him when we met.'

'Already engaged?' Luca's fork clattered to his plate. His mouth gaped in shock. 'But you still are, if the vicar is expecting you and him to discuss weddings on Saturday! I don't understand. You didn't tell me. Why didn't you say anything?'

Lauren stared at him dumbly, her pale face lit by two bright pink spots.

Roberto stirred at last. 'Presumably we're talking about Ewen Walkis?' he said, twisting towards Beth. 'The guy you told me about.'

'Beth!' Lauren turned on her. 'You didn't. You promised you wouldn't say anything.'

'I didn't!' Beth protested, feeling as if she was being squeezed on all sides. 'Not about you and him being engaged. His name just kept cropping up all the time.'

Support came from the most unexpected source. 'Beth's telling you the truth,' Roberto told Lauren. 'Whenever anyone mentioned Ewen Walkis' name, your sister did her utmost to change the subject. Now I realise why . . . ' he added under his breath.

'Sorry, Beth,' said Lauren, chewing her lip. Her face was so small and pale and anguished, Beth's heart went out to her. Reality seemed to have crashed in on her at last, and she was floundering for a foothold. She couldn't leave her struggling.

Beth started to speak, but Lauren halted her. 'No, I really am sorry, Beth. It's no good trying to make excuses for me. I'm in the wrong. I have been from the start. You kept telling me that. I've been an absolute idiot.' She got up and went over to Luca. 'I'm sorry. I should have told you.'

Luca stood up uncertainly. 'Yes, you should have.'

Beth could see he was at a loss to know how to deal with the sudden change in the situation. The couple had reached a make or break moment.

'I know.' Lauren rubbed her face while shaking her head. 'And I'm really sorry, Luca. I can't give you an excuse . . . because . . . because I just don't have one.'

He made to push past her, but she caught his arm. 'Where are you going?'

'Where am I going? You don't expect me to stay . . . ?'

The spots on Lauren's cheeks flared. 'If you're leaving in a huff, you can't have loved me very much in the first place!'

'What about you!' Luca exploded. 'Lying to me from the beginning . . . '

'I didn't lie. Not exactly. I just didn't tell you!'

Beth made to rise. Roberto's hand on her arm slowed her momentarily. He was signalling to her to allow them to sort it out between themselves. But she brushed him aside and stood up.

'If there's going to be a row, I'd rather it not be in here. Not with Major unwell at the moment.' She was desperate for them not to argue at all, but in a way Roberto was right. It was up to them now.

Luca stalked off into the hall, with Lauren following. Their raised voices drifted through, but thankfully they both seemed under control.

'I knew this had to come,' cried Beth, sinking back down into her chair. She felt like she'd been spun through a mangle.

Roberto's hand squeezing her shoulder was like a shot of electricity surging through her.

'I knew something wasn't right,' he said, twisting his chair to face her. 'I just didn't expect that.'

'Will Luca be okay?' she asked.

He breathed in sharply. 'I'd say his pride is dented, but I don't believe his heart is broken. He'll get over it . . .'

She nodded slowly, sensing he was right, drawing calm from his mood. She'd suspected all along it was just attraction, infatuation, on both sides, something that would fade as quickly as it had arrived. But why did Lauren have to get so carried away?

'So what happens now?' he asked thoughtfully.

'Who knows? From tonight I think I've officially given up wondering what Lauren will do next . . . '

'I didn't mean with Lauren — ' he began, shaking his head before apparently changing tack again. 'This explains why I've felt all along you've been holding out on me.'

'Holding out?' she echoed, not quite meeting his eyes.

'Holding back on me then.'

'I'm sorry,' she murmured faintly. If he only knew how difficult it had been. How it had cast a shadow over every second of the last couple of days.

'You could have told me, you know.' His voice was as low as hers. 'I wish you'd felt able to trust me, Beth.'

'But it was Lauren's secret. I gave her my word I wouldn't say anything to anyone until she could tell Ewen. Aren't I the fool!' she added wryly.

His hand darted out and took hers.

'You're not a fool, Beth. You're a loyal sister trying to do the right thing.'

'Like you are with your cousin,' she said, licking her dry lips before continuing. 'Roberto, I'm sorry about this morning, accusing you like that. I don't know how I came to that conclusion . . .'

Actually, she did. It was the pain talking.

Because she'd fallen hopelessly, irrevocably in love with Roberto and knew it to be a lost cause. Apart from being on the wrong foot with him from the very beginning, discovering what different worlds they lived in had dashed any tiny germ of hope that there could ever be something of lasting significance between them.

That same pain was needling through her body now, at the thought of him leaving. Never ever seeing him again.

While they'd been talking, the conversation in the hall had dried up. As one set of footsteps suddenly thudded rapidly up the stairs, Lauren burst into the kitchen, looking stricken.

'Are you okay?' asked Beth. 'What's happening now?'

'We're finished,' she said dully. 'Luca's gone up to pack and — ' She stopped, because the back door had suddenly opened and a man walked in.

'Ewen!' Lauren gasped. 'Oh, my gosh! You weren't due back until Friday.'

Beth scrambled to her feet, aware that Roberto was also standing up.

Ewen still stood on the threshold. 'I had an anonymous text message suggesting it was in my interests to come back early . . . '

Beth drew in her breath and glanced at Roberto. Could he have sent it? But she dismissed the idea as quickly as it had arrived. For one thing, he wouldn't have Ewen's phone number.

'There's some stupid rumour doing the rounds, Lauren, about you seeing someone else . . . ?' Ewen's eyes flickered questioningly at Roberto.

Beth gave a small shake of her head.

Her heart went out to Ewen. His usually clear blue eyes were clouded with doubt. She could tell he was desperate for Lauren to deny the rumour, laugh it off, make his world okay again. But she couldn't, could she?

'Ewen — ' Beth began, tentatively holding out her hand.

'Leave it,' Roberto murmured severely in her ear.

Her annoyance was short-lived. He was right. She'd nearly done it again. But she'd given up fighting Lauren's battles for her.

'We'll leave you to talk in private,' said Roberto, and with his arm loosely around her shoulder, steered Beth to the door.

'I'm not going any further,' she protested when they'd entered the hall. 'Just in case . . . '

The tone of the voices coming from the other side of the kitchen door were more distressed than angry.

Beth sank down onto the stairs, her head in her hands.

Wordlessly, Roberto went into the dining room, and returned with two small glasses of rich-coloured liquid. 'Cognac,' he said, handing one to her.

'I don't drink the stuff.'

'Drink it,' he said. 'You need something. In fact, we both do. It's been what you'd call a bit of an evening!' He downed his, and watched as, with a splutter, she managed to finish hers.

Then he prised the glass from her fingers and put it down beside his on a narrow side table. 'I'm just going up to check on Luca,' he said, brushing past her and bounding up the stairs two at a time. 'Don't go away!'

She wasn't going anywhere.

The kitchen door opened and Lauren ran down the hall, tears streaming down her face. As Beth stood up, Lauren darted round her and up the stairs.

Ewen emerged from the kitchen. He looked close to tears himself. He gazed at Beth wordlessly.

'Oh, Ewen . . . ' she whispered, going over to him.

She'd known him forever, right from their days together at the village primary and junior schools, although he'd been a few years behind her. 'It'll be all right. She's seen sense now. She loves you really. She always did. She just lost her head over a romantic fantasy . . . '

'She thinks she can go back to how we were, like nothing happened. I've had to break off our engagement, Beth. Even if it's breaking my own heart to do it. I think it's called cutting off your nose to spite your face . . . '

His attempt at humour collapsed into a choke, and suddenly he was sobbing his heart out.

'Don't, Ewen,' she said, consoling him with a hug. 'I know you still love her, even if you can't stand the sight of her at the moment. But it'll all work itself out, you'll see . . . ' She wished she felt as confident as she sounded.

'I'm sorry, Beth,' he said, struggling

and eventually regaining control.

'Just give yourself some time to cool off and think straight. You and Lauren both need to do that. Okay, Ewen?'

He leaned back and surveyed her briefly, before pressing a kiss to her cheek. 'You're right. You always were the best. Thanks, Bessie.'

She pulled a face at his use of her old playground name, though she didn't think he even knew he'd done it. After closing the front door after him, she paused with her hand on the wood, as if she could draw some strength from something reassuringly solid in what had become an unstable world. Things were clearing though, weren't they? She had an inkling that Lauren and Ewen might even get back together eventually, given time. Luca would be okay, and Roberto — ?

She turned to find him standing on the bottom step, staring directly at her. To say he looked furious was an understatement.

11

Icy panic trickled through Beth's veins as she walked quickly up to Roberto at the foot of the stairs. 'Oh, no, please don't say Luca's done something stupid . . . ?' It was the only thing she could imagine which would account for his Roberto's anger.

'Luca's fine,' he barked coldly, while his eyes glittered. 'But I can hear your sister crying her eyes out?'

'I'll go to her.' She made to go round him, but he neatly side-stepped in front of her. What was wrong with him? 'Excuse me,' she said, lifting her head. She might not have spoken.

'Seeing what I've just witnessed,' he said, his hand darting out and encircling her wrist, 'I don't blame her for being upset. Does she know?'

'Know what?' Mystified, she tried to pull her arm away. His hold felt so secure and yet his touch was as soft as velvet.

'That you were all for her marrying Luca because it would leave Ewen Walkis free for you.'

'What!' Was she meant to laugh? He was joking, of course. But he wasn't. His face was a mask of conflicting emotions — and humour very definitely wasn't one of them.

Her stomach churned uncontrollably. The lingering taste of cognac burned on her tongue, making her feel physically nauseous. Struggling to manage her own feelings of astonishment and indignation she could hardly begin to imagine what was in his mind.

Swallowing hard, she tossed back her head. 'You're crazy. How could you accuse me of such a thing?' Yet even as she said it she was remembering how readily she'd flung her own hurtful and unfounded accusation at him. Is that what he was doing — getting his own back?

She couldn't believe he could be as

petty as that. But then if it wasn't vengeance making sparks flash from his eyes, or his jaw tighten so visibly, then what was it?

'Because I saw you together just now.' His voice was suddenly very controlled, very harsh.

'But there was nothing to see,' she protested. 'I was just comforting him over Lauren. He's devastated, the poor lamb.'

'Poor lamb! Is that your special name for him? Like he calls you Bessie?'

She winced. 'I hate being called Bessie — and Ewen knows it. When he was five and his front teeth fell out, he developed a lisp and couldn't pronounce my name properly . . . ' Oh, why was she even bothering to tell him all this? He clearly didn't believe her.

She jerked her arm backwards, and this time managed to dislodge his hold. 'This is stupid. Lauren's out of Luca's life, which is what you wanted all along. So none of this is anything to do with you any more — '

She stopped, because he'd rocked back on his heels. Yet he recovered so quickly she wondered if she'd imagined it. When he spoke his eyes widened, apparently blacker and deeper than ever. 'No, you're right. It's none of my business. But I feel you ought to know — assuming you're interested of course — that he's not in love with you.'

She gasped. And Roberto started to turn, as if to make his way back upstairs. She stared at him, dumbfounded for a second. Why make such a ludicrous comment? And then to turn his back on her?

'Why on earth would I think that Ewen's in love with me?' she demanded. Before she knew what she was doing, she leapt up onto the bottom step, her hand on his arm to stop him walking away. 'For that matter, what's it to you anyway?'

He twisted back. Squeezed together on the same step now, but still she had to look up at him. She noticed the movement in his shoulders, uncertain whether it was a shrug or a tremor of tension.

'I just wouldn't want you to read something more significant than fondness into that kiss the two of you just shared.'

'Oh, it wasn't a kiss,' she snapped. 'Not in that sense. But then I guess you know far more about the subject of kissing than me!'

'Too right I do — '

Something in his voice sent her heart into overdrive. She made a conscious effort to try to slow down her breathing, but it was useless. She stared at him, determined to hold his gaze directly, not to shy away. Not to move away. Not this time. They were standing so very close together. Her shoes were toe to toe with his. She couldn't move away — not even if she wanted to.

' — and just so you know the difference in future, this is what I call a lovers' kiss — '

His lips met hers in a feverish and angry crush.

A rush of hot emotion flooded every part of her. She raised her palms against his chest, intending to use his body to ease herself away. Through the crisp cotton of his shirt, his heart was beating like fury. Her traitorous arms though, instead of pushing him away, seemed intent on moving round to his back and pulling him to her. At the same time, his arms were sweeping around to encircle her, gathering her up and drawing her ever closer to him. The kiss went on, deeper and deeper. It was a kiss she never wanted to end. Even when her lungs felt completely exhausted, she had never in her life before felt so alive.

When they finally broke apart she was gasping for air.

'I — I — ' she began. She didn't have much of an idea what she was going to say, but the sound of a door opening above threw her completely. It distracted Roberto too, enough for his grip to loosen. She took the opportunity to duck past him and up, surprised that her legs — in their current wool-like state — were capable of holding her upright, let alone mounting a flight of stairs.

'Coming, Lauren,' she called, her voice little more than a quavery warble.

Turning the corner at the top, and not hearing Roberto's steps behind her, she leaned against the landing wall in an attempt to gather herself. Lauren must have gone to the bathroom; she could hear the sound of water running.

Beth put her palms to her cheeks. But it wasn't just her face, her whole body was zinging. The Roberto effect. She'd known it, hadn't he? Known all along, from that very first glance across the airport, that this man should come with a health warning. She should have heeded her own advice, instead of throwing herself at him like that, responding so totally.

If she suspected her own feelings were on the point of no return before, that kiss had just set the seal on everything — for her at least. Her heart would never be the same again.

Did he know, she wondered with a sob, just how completely and utterly she'd fallen in love with him? And if he did, did he even care? No, of course not. As far as he was concerned, she was after Ewen. How Roberto squared that with the way she'd responded to his kiss she had no idea. Unless he just needed to prove how irresistible he was, and how insincere Beth was in her feelings. A renewed sense of being judged unfairly coiled up in her. But what was the point? It was all so completely hopeless.

Dashing away her tears, she stumbled along the corridor and tapped on the bathroom door. 'Lauren. Lauren, let me in.'

Lauren was pressing cold water to her own reddened, tear-streaked face. She met Beth's face in the mirror with alarm. 'You look worse than me!'

'Thanks!' She handed Lauren a towel, and perched on the edge of the bath. 'I'm fine. Do you want to talk about it yet?'

Lauren shrugged, but then dissolved into fresh tears. Beth gave her a hug.

'Thanks for not saying 'I told you so',' mumbled Lauren.

Beth didn't feel comfortable accepting the compliment; it had been on the very tip of her tongue. 'So what happens now?'

'I give Ewen his ring back. Let Kevin know the wedding's off.' She stepped back, sat down on the loo seat and blew her nose. 'Oh, Beth, why have I been such an idiot? Do you think Ewen will ever forgive me?'

'I honestly don't know, Beth. You've hurt him very badly. That you're kicking yourself is probably no consolation at the moment. You'll just have to wait and see if he comes round in time.'

'He didn't even let me tell him how it happened. It was all so romantic, being in Italy. I think I fell in love with the idea of falling in love at first sight. And there was Luca, across a crowded room and all that. But you were right all along, it was all just a stupid illusion. We started getting on each other's nerves after only a few days. We're the same age, but he seems years younger than me . . . how on earth could I have ever thought I loved him? As soon as I saw Ewen tonight I knew . . . ' She broke off only to take a deep sigh.

'You warned me I'd probably end up losing both of them, didn't you? But Ewen's the only one I want. And it's only now I've lost him I realise just how much he means to me.'

From staring into the middle distance, she suddenly focussed on Beth's face. 'What's up?' She reached out a hand. 'It's not just all the aggravation I've caused you that's making you look like that?'

Beth shook her head and attempted a smile. '*Just* all the aggravation,' she teased.

Lauren lips curved ruefully. 'But seriously — it's not Major, is it? He's going to be okay, isn't he?'

'I'm sure he's going to be fine. Though I'll need to go back down and check up on him.' Beth stood up, then hesitated. 'Will you come with me, Lauren? Only Roberto might still be prowling around and — ' Beth's explanation faltered. She couldn't think of any excuse but the truth. ' — and I really can't face bumping into him right now.'

'Did he give you a hard time over me?'

'No. No, he didn't. It's just we've had a bit of a misunderstanding over a couple of things today . . . and I find him a bit — um — unpredictable,' she finished lamely, wishing she'd never started explaining at all.

'You haven't been winding him up, have you?'

'Me!' Beth gasped. 'More the other way round.'

Lauren chuckled with a knowing air. 'I think it must be you. You bring out his Italian temperament!'

Down in the kitchen, Lauren fussed

over Major. 'You're looking brighter already, aren't you, boy! Can he have some food tonight, do you think?'

Nodding, Beth went to the cupboard. 'Fleur said he could have his normal meal, as long as he wanted it.'

'He does. His tail's thumping!'

While Beth fed him, Lauren boiled the kettle. 'I'm taking up some tea. Want some?'

'Please.' Beth cleared the table and started to tidy up. No-one had eaten very much at all. Glancing at the clock, she was surprised to see it was only just after ten o'clock. She'd be glad to go up to bed early herself.

'There you go,' said Lauren, sliding a mug across the worktop, before picking up her own. 'You coming up now too?'

'I'll just finish checking round.'

'Okay. I might try sending Ewen a quick text. Or do you think I should leave it for tonight — ?'

'There doesn't appear to be any mobile signal at the moment.'

Beth started as Roberto appeared in

the doorway. He held up his blank phone as if to prove his reason for being there. 'I've come down to use the landline if I may? Or the computer. I need to check flight times and book tickets.'

'Of course. You know where the office is.' She didn't intend sounding so waspish, but to her dismay that was how her words came out. Roberto's slightly anguished reaction told her that. But the thought of him leaving hurt so much.

For a mad second she toyed with the wild idea of telling him how she felt. It was such a silly notion that she had to stifle an almost hysterical burst of laughter. The sound caused his eyes to lock on her again. Biting her lip, she quickly turned her head away.

Tell him she was in love with him! It was unbearable to think of the impressions he would already be taking away of her. A scruffy, disorganised English woman; suspicious, defensive, rude, forgetful, chaotic, a poor hostess, prone to making snap and erroneous judgements — and to cap it all, intent on hooking her sister's original fiancé! That was enough of a list without adding romantic delusional to it!

But then what else should he expect, kissing her like that. She pressed her fingers to her lips. She'd defy any woman not to fall in love after a kiss like that. And how many other women had? Probably too many for Roberto to remember. If that was the case, then she needn't worry about what sort of impression of her he'd go away with; he'd probably never give the last few days another second's thought.

Yet she would never, ever, forget them.

Beth swerved the opposite way round the central island so she didn't have to pass him as he strode towards the office.

Clearly he was desperate to get back to Italy and resume his usual lifestyle.

'I'm not surprised Luca wants to go home as soon as possible,' Lauren said, sounding embarrassed and contrite at the same time. 'I'm sorry, Roberto. You've been really understanding about us all along.'

Beth's stomach flipped, even though the smile he gave was for Lauren.

'I'm sorry that it didn't work out between you two — ' he broke off momentarily, ' — even if your sister doesn't believe me on that point.'

Beth felt Lauren's enquiring eyes switch onto her.

'I think I'll go straight up after all,' Beth told her, miraculously achieving the impossible by giving the impression that Roberto wasn't there, let alone disturbing her so much. 'Major's settled back in his basket for the night. Can you switch off and lock up?'

Without looking back, she fled up the stairs, needing the space and solitude of her own room, to think, to breathe. And to cry her heart out.

12

When Beth got out of bed and pulled back the curtains, the dawn was just streaking the sky with beautiful shades of turquoise and lemon. She hadn't really slept at all, but now the day had begun properly, it hit her: Roberto was leaving today.

Pulling on jeans and a jumper, she crept quickly downstairs. There was a risk she would bump into him, but she had to take it. She needed to see how Major was.

The aroma of coffee that met her in the hall warned her she was not the first person up.

'Morning, Beth,' Roberto said, sounding far too chirpy for her liking. But then he was happy, wasn't he? Now this hiatus was coming to an end.

He collected her favourite mug from the shelf and took it over to the coffee machine. 'Sleep well?'

She mumbled non-commitally. Surely he could see she looked absolutely wrecked. Typically he was as poised and immaculately-groomed as usual. Clearly he'd not spent a restless night, either worrying about Luca, or reliving over and over again every nuance of that kiss on the stairs.

'Pardon?'

She lifted her head momentarily. 'Yes, good, thanks. You?'

Without waiting for an answer, she bent down to greet Major in his basket.

Roberto left the coffee machine and came to squat down beside her. 'He seems fine this morning. I got up early in case he wanted to go out, but he didn't. Perhaps he was waiting for you,' he added, as Major did now stir, his tail wagging eagerly.

'I'm glad it's dry today,' she said briskly, following the dog and opening the door to outside. 'Fleur said to keep the foot bandage dry, which will mean covering it in polythene when it rains. I can't see him being very keen on that indignity . . . ' From the corner of her eye, she caught Roberto's raised eyebrows.

Of course she'd no need to tell him what the vet had said because he'd been there with her at the time — as if Beth would ever forget it. But at least it kept the conversation away from what was uppermost in her mind; last night's kiss and his imminent departure.

She picked up her coffee and stood by the door, leaning on the frame and watching Major potter round the courtyard area. It was no good. She didn't want to know, yet she had to. 'What time are your flights leaving?'

She'd wanted it to seem a cool, impartial enquiry, but of course it would come out sounding anxious and breathless.

'Late morning — '

His voice was close, but she didn't turn round, didn't want him to see her pained expression.

'Don't worry,' he added, 'we'll soon

be out of your hair.'

His words twisted like a knife. She didn't want him out of her hair, her life, or anything else. But even if he could see that, it wouldn't matter to him, would it?

Did she have any ignominy left to lose by telling him how she felt? She found herself turning round after all, to stare at him. He was cutting slices from the loaf she'd bought yesterday. 'I think that might be a bit stale.'

'It'll be fine for toast.'

'Will you need a lift?' she began. 'Because — '

Because it would mean an extra couple of hours in his company at least. She couldn't bear him leaving with the idea that she was any way interested romantically in Ewen. And even if she couldn't convince him of that, she still wanted to be as long in his company as possible, despite how excruciatingly awkward that might be.

'Thank you, Beth, but no. I'll be driving myself. I've arranged to drop off the hire car at the airport.'

'Oh.' That was a good thing, really, wasn't it? Saving her from herself. And it would only have prolonged the torture. Not to mention a public goodbye at the airport. That would have been truly unbearable. It was going to be agony as it was. For her, anyway. Had that kiss really meant nothing to him other than to prove a point? Her lips were still tingling with the memory. Her heart would remain bruised for a whole lot longer.

'Beth. About yesterday evening,' he began, taking a step towards her. 'I'm sorry if I . . . if you . . . ?'

'I know, the heat of the moment and all that,' she interrupted quickly, blushing furiously, and desperate not to have to endure him attempting to let her down gently.

'It's been a whirlwind few days, really, hasn't it? Still,' she swept on briskly, 'it's all over now. You must be desperate to get back home. Now there's nothing to keep you here, I mean. It'll be good to get back to normal, won't it? No doubt you've got places to go, people to see . . . ' She managed a droll little shrug. 'I know I have! Life goes on, doesn't it . . . ?' She was babbling utter rubbish now.

He blinked slowly. 'Hmm, something like that, yes.' He popped in the bread and twisted the dial on the toaster. 'Sure you won't have any?'

'No. Not just now, thanks.' She managed to turn away before her tears started to fall. And stepping outside into the garden, she went to follow Major.

It was a beautiful morning. The gentle warmth in the sun, the chattering birds, the sticky buds on the trees. All of nature was shouting 'Spring!', but in her heart, it felt like the end of everything.

When she brought Major back inside to give him his breakfast, the kitchen was empty. Presumably Roberto had gone to roust up Luca, and to pack. He really couldn't wait to get away, could he?

'I still can't get any response from Ewen,' said Lauren, when she trailed into the kitchen, her face pale and with deep blue hollows under her eyes. 'His mobile's switched off and there's no answer from the farmhouse either.'

Beth took a sip of coffee. 'Perhaps he's gone back to finish his course.'

'Do you think so? But how could he concentrate when we've just split up?'

'It might take his mind off it. He was pretty upset when he left here last night.'

Lauren dropped down into a kitchen chair and sunk her head into her hands. 'Do you think he'll ever forgive me? Perhaps I'll just drive over to the farm anyway. If he is there, he might be prepared to hear me out today.' She lifted her head, a hopeful spark coming into her eyes.

'Talk him round, you mean!' Privately, Beth thought it would take more than a few hours for Ewen to get over the shock, let alone begin to think about forgiving her, but then Lauren always could wrap him round her little finger. Beth sighed. What did she know really? She was hardly the expert on love and relationships.

'Okay,' she told Lauren, 'but not just yet. Can you hold fire for a bit? Roberto and Luca are leaving soon. You can't just swan off and not even say goodbye.'

Beth left Lauren chasing unwanted cornflakes around a bowl, while she went outside and got on with a few jobs in the greenhouse. She could see Roberto's hired Mercedes from there.

It was true what she said; life did go on. There was a weekend residential course starting Friday and she was a long way behind with the usual preparations. With the accommodation to prepare and the catering to finalise, there was plenty to do inside the Lodge, but as ever, the outside work called her first. She was up to her wrists in compost when the light flashed on the house phone extension she'd had installed in the greenhouse.

She decided to leave the answer-phone to kick in, but it stopped flashing after a few seconds, so she guessed Lauren had picked up. Perhaps it was Ewen calling her anyway, if he couldn't get through on her mobile.

Was it possible they would get past this hiccup and marry after all? Perhaps it boiled down to trust at the end of the day. Ewen had to be certain that Lauren truly loved him. Or was his love so strong that he'd take a chance on her anyway?

Whoever it was on the phone, the call didn't last long, and Beth got on with pricking out summer bedding seedlings into large trays.

'Beth . . . it's Ewen!' Seconds later, Lauren came stumbling into the green-house, her face as white as a sheet and barely able to get her words out. 'He's had an accident and just been rushed into Casualty!'

'Oh my gosh! How serious is it?' Dropping her tools, and hastily brush-ing the worst of the compost off on her jeans, Beth dashed back to the house, with Lauren running at her side. 'What did they say exactly?'

'That he'd had a fall. From the loft in the barn, I think. I can't remember properly. Oh, Beth, what am I going to do if anything's happened to him . . . it's all my fault . . . '

'Okay, let's keep calm. We'll go straight up to the hospital. They're bound to give us more information when we get there.'

She paused in the kitchen only to check that Major was settled in his basket, and to grab her phone, bag and van keys. 'Right, let's go.'

As they headed out through the hall, Roberto was coming down the stairs, clad in jeans and a shirt. No suit today, which wasn't surprising. It had been ruined in the rain yesterday, soaked through and covered with ditch mud. And she hadn't even offered to get it cleaned. Well it was too late now. He was carrying his and Luca's holdalls, and his camera bag. Everything packed and all ready to leave. This was it. Beth's heart nosedived.

Roberto stopped on the last step. Beth wondered if he realised the significance of that spot.

'What's happened?' he asked, glancing at both their faces.

Lauren quickly told him about Ewen's accident, blushing at the mention of his name as she glanced at Luca.

Roberto took the final step down into the hall, dropping the bags onto the floor. 'Is there anything I can do?'

'I don't think so. But thank you,' Beth added. 'We're going to the hospital now.'

Luca moved forwards, and Lauren hovered on her heels. Beth wondered how this awkward farewell would go. In the end they both smiled almost sheepishly, shared the briefest of hugs, and wished each other good luck for the future.

With a shy goodbye for Beth, Luca picked up his holdall and headed for the door.

'Can we go now, Beth?' Lauren urged her anxiously.

'Are you sure I can't do anything to help?' Roberto turned to ask.

'No, it's fine.' The last of the quartet to leave the Lodge, she pulled the large front door shut behind her. 'Really. You'll miss your flights.'

Turning, she saw Luca getting into the Mercedes. Lauren was belting up in the Toyota.

Much, much closer, Roberto was gazing softly at her. 'What — ?' she said, raising her hand to her face, she felt grit on her skin. The potting compost. His last sight of her was very much resembling his first; scruffy and unglamorous. Exasperated, she made to rub the dirt away, but Roberto got there first. 'Here, allow me.'

His hand cupped her chin, and stayed there. She felt hypnotized by his eyes, staring deeper and deeper into hers. Then slowly his fingers began to caress her skin.

They spoke over each other.

'Roberto — '

'Beth, perhaps we could — '

Talking over each other, both their voices were cut off by twin blasts from the Toyota's and the Mercedes' horns.

'I must go. Lauren's desperate to get the hospital as soon as possible,' she explained, 'and I couldn't let her drive her own car, not in the state she's in.'

His lips curved in a now familiar soft smile. 'No, I know.' He nodded thoughtfully. 'And Luca's anxious not to miss our flights.'

'Have a safe journey, a good trip . . . ' Have a good life, she added silently, gulping back a sob. No way was she going to break down in front of him. And no way could she survive a farewell embrace. She turned away abruptly and fled to the van.

It started first time and she roared away up the drive without a backward glance. Lauren looked at her in surprise. 'You've not done up your seatbelt — ?'

She fastened it before exiting the

drive, while waiting for a gap in the traffic, and then turned left heading towards the hospital at Norwich. In the rear view mirror, she caught the briefest glimpse of the silver Mercedes, travelling in the opposite direction. Every second, every minute, every hour from then on would take them further and further apart.

The old saying 'ships that pass in the night' came to mind. She desperately wanted to pull over into a lay-by and cry her heart out, but Lauren's anxiety, and the thought of Ewen laying there injured in hospital, kept her foot to the accelerator. The familiar mechanics of driving brought a certain, welcome calm.

And Lauren wanted to talk.

'I really love Ewen, you know. What on earth came over me in Italy? If only we hadn't had that stupid row over it. I should never have gone by myself, should I? I can't believe I hurt him so badly. And now he's had an accident and it's all my fault. He was probably tired and distracted and lost concentration.'

'We don't know how it happened yet,' Beth murmured, 'and there's no point beating yourself up about it.'

It was as if Lauren hadn't heard her. 'He'd driven all that way back yesterday evening after getting that text. That was my fault too. Parading Luca round town like a new pair of shoes! Anyone could have seen us. It was bound to get back to Ewen.'

After a while, Lauren shuffled awkwardly in the passenger seat. 'Luca and I, we never — ' she began awkwardly, ' — you know, actually slept together — '

'It's your life, Lauren,' Beth interrupted. 'You really don't have to justify yourself me.'

'I know, but I want you to know, so you don't think any worse of me than you already do.'

Beth glanced at her and tutted. 'Don't be daft! You're my sister. If I've been getting on at you it's only because I love you and want the best for you.'

'I know. Thanks, sis.' Lauren's voice was choked. 'And I guess it's Ewen I have to convince now. I just hope he's going to be all right . . . '

'Of course he will be . . . ' Beth suddenly noticed something. 'Hey, you've got Ewen's engagement ring back on!'

'You know what hospitals are like about needing to know who you are before giving you any information. And if I can't convince them I'm Ewen's fiancée, then what hope have I got of convincing him!'

'Honestly, Lauren!' Smiling, Beth shook her head. 'Trust you to think of everything!'

The drive to Norwich had never seemed so far. 'Come on, lights, change . . . change . . . ' Beth tapped the steering wheel while they waited at a red signal. She glanced down, and noticed a CD case in the groove by the handbrake. She didn't usually play music or even listen to the radio while driving. The van always made such a racket it was impossible to hear anything properly.

'Is that one of yours?' she asked.

Lauren picked up the CD and turned it over. 'Mario somebody? Nope. Never heard of him. I'm not into all that jazz and soul stuff, am I.'

No, of course she wasn't. But it rung a bell with Beth now. It was the album playing in the car coming back from the vet's, the Italian singer she'd admired so much. But how on earth had it got in the Toyota — unless Roberto had left it there for her? A memento of a time she could never forget.

13

Beth carefully balanced two steaming coffee mugs by their handles in one hand, while she rapped on the door with the other. 'Are you ever going to come out of that bathroom!'

'Okay, okay, keep your hair on!' The door opened and there stood a grinning Lauren, muffled in a pink dressing gown, her head wrapped in a matching fluffy towel, the whole ensemble surrounded by an invisible cloud of perfume. 'I've been having the most wonderfully relaxing bath.'

Beth wished she could feel half as calm. 'But you've not even done your face yet,' she cried in alarm, handing over one of the coffees.

'Thanks. Well, I can't, can I? Not before I get into my dress. I don't want to get make-up all over it. Don't panic, there's plenty of time . . . '

'Not all that much time. Don't forget I know what you're like when you're getting ready to go anywhere!'

Lauren stuck her tongue out. 'Well at least I haven't got to wonder about what I'm going to wear!'

In her room, Lauren closed the door so they could both gaze on the full-length traditional white satin gown hanging behind it.

'It's gorgeous,' breathed Beth, putting her coffee well to one side before reaching up to take it down.

She had to clear a space to lay it flat on the bed. Lauren's room had its usual appearance of a tornado having just blown through it, but the mess today comprised mainly of temporary ephemera; good luck cards, wrapping paper, balloons and some pre-emptive confetti. A huge vase of fat red roses occupied most of the dressing table, their scent mingled with the warm summer air drifting in through the open window. Apart from Lauren's make-up and hairdryer and other bits and pieces, all her other personal items had already been transported over to Ewen's farmhouse cottage, ready for when she moved in after they got back from their honeymoon.

'It is gorgeous, isn't it?' Lauren stroked the dress through its protective polythene. 'I only hope Ewen thinks so too.'

'You'll knock his eyes out,' whispered Beth. 'Come on, drink that coffee, and then let's get you into it.'

Beth was still slightly awestruck that the wedding was taking place at all, let alone to the original timescale. That was when she had time to think about it. Since the spring, everything had been crazily hectic. Right from Ewen's accident, from which he'd fortunately recovered quickly, helped by Lauren's tender loving care. She'd thrown herself into lending a hand around the farm, and getting involved in the conservation work that was not only his livelihood but his passion. It hadn't been just a matter of convincing him of her love, she'd shown by her dedication how much she regretted her impulsive and downright stupid Italian engagement.

Both of them had agreed to put the episode behind them, and on Ewen's part, to forgive and forget. It was the sensible way to go. That was how Ewen had put it when he'd confided in Beth. Otherwise how could they ever go forward? He was right, of course.

But Beth could never forget about those few days. She felt as strongly about Roberto Di Ferraio now as she had on the day they'd parted.

At least they'd kept in touch since then, albeit only by phone, but it was more than Beth could have dared to hope for.

The day he'd left, when she'd come out of the hospital for a breather, leaving Lauren at Ewen's bedside, she'd switched her mobile back on and found a text message from Roberto asking her to call him when she could.

Before she could talk herself out of it, she'd rung his number, but it had gone to voicemail. She'd sat on a bench in the hospital grounds, just as a plane had gone over. It wasn't the one he was on, of course, but he was probably somewhere mid-air at that very moment, with his phone switched off. So she'd left a message with brief details of Ewen's condition, although nerves got the better of her and typically she made a hash of it. And then she forgot to thank him for the Mario Biondi CD, and so dithered for ages over whether to ring back and leave another message, or wait to see if he responded to the first one.

But what if he didn't? Annoyed with herself for behaving like a scatty schoolgirl, she left another quick message. It wasn't until she was back home that evening she discovered she'd had a text message simply saying, 'My pleasure.'

She was disappointed it wasn't a voice mail. But then she would only have spent too long replaying it over and over.

It was a few days later, while she was occupied outside, giving the newly arrived set of weekend course residents a tour of the garden, that her phone rang. Glancing briefly at the screen, and not recognising the number, she said a brisk, 'Hello, may I call you back in a moment?'

There was a brief hesitation down the line, then, 'Okay, Beth.' It was such a shock to hear Roberto's rich brown voice, as clear as a bell, as if he'd been standing there in the flesh and murmuring in her ear, that she all but dropped the phone. By the time she'd juggled it and returned it to her ear, he'd rung off.

She wanted to ring him straight back, but the group were waiting expectantly.

It was twenty minutes later, when they'd all returned to the Lodge and were busy bonding over coffee and biscuits around the kitchen table with an eager Major in attendance, that she could slip out to the hall with the house phone in her hand. Her heart was beating wildly as she waited for his number to ring.

'Hi.'

Just that one word and her whole body shook. She slid down and perched on the bottom stair.

'Hi — ' she responded, before her mind went completely blank.

'Beth? Are you still there?'

'Yes, yes. Sorry I couldn't talk earlier. I was busy showing round a group of people. Was it important?' she asked faintly, holding her breath.

'Important?'

'Why you called?'

'Oh, yes. Yes, it was, actually . . . I wanted to know how Major was getting on.'

'Oh. Very well. Fleur had another look at him yesterday. His paw is healing up fine, no trace of infection, thank goodness. The bandage is off now too, which has cheered him up no end.'

He chuckled. 'That's good news. No lasting damage.'

'No, thank goodness. He's now

happily scrounging for biscuits from the people here for the weekend course.'

'Really, the traitor! How can he have forgotten me so soon?'

'We haven't,' she replied softly and quickly. She could see Roberto now in her mind's eye, feeding pieces of ham to Major in the kitchen. 'I mean, he hasn't . . . ' There was so much she wanted to say, but she still couldn't find a way, or pluck up the courage, to express how she felt.

Instead she asked, 'Are your hands okay now? Those scratches healing up properly?'

'Hmm. Without a scar, you mean? Not so you'd notice,' he added.

The remark perplexed her slightly. But she was distracted by the sudden mental picture of his smooth, strong hands and fingers.

He asked about Ewen, and she updated him on his accident and injuries. 'He lost his footing while he was working in one of the barn lofts at the farm. He's suffered several cracked ribs, a fractured shoulder, and concussion. But he's going to be all right. Lauren's up at the hospital with him most of the time. He should be out in a day or two though.'

They talked a little more, with Beth asking after Luca and his mother.

'She's having another little flutter, I'm afraid, since Luca announced he's going travelling over the summer.'

'Oh, dear. It's not his disappointment over Lauren that's driven him to that, is it?'

'No, don't worry on that score. It was something he was talking about before he met her and decided he wanted to be a young husband instead!' His exasperated sigh floated down the line.

Beth, the phone tucked close under her hair, hugged her knees to herself and smiled. She could listen to Roberto's voice all day

'Will you have to go travelling too, to keep an eye on him?'

'Not likely. I'm too old for backpacking. And I doubt if he and his friends want me cramping their style anyway. Besides, I'm too busy. I've got urgent plans of my own to follow up . . . '

He left a pause, as if inviting her to ask what they were, but she just didn't dare. A nagging voice in the back of her brain kept suggesting his plans might involve Leola.

'Beth? Are you still there?'

'Hmm.'

'Look, this is awkward, over the phone. I'd rather we spoke about it face to face, but I guess it shouldn't wait. About that last evening . . . '

The evening of the kiss on the stairs. If he wanted to discuss that, she was glad he wasn't there in person to see the warmth in her face. 'Yes?' she breathed.

'When I accused you of wanting Ewen. It was a ridiculous idea, and I apologise for thinking it, let alone saying it.'

'It's okay,' she replied. 'I wanted to apologise properly to you too. For saying what I did in the car, about you thinking Lauren wasn't good enough for your family. I had no justification for that.'

A short silence stretched across the miles.

'All forgiven and forgotten then,' he said.

'All forgiven and forgotten,' she echoed.

'So how do things stand between Ewen and Lauren now?'

'I'm quite hopeful they'll get back together eventually. They probably will, if Lauren's got any say in the matter. She can be very persuasive.'

His laugh came down the line. 'Let me know if they do get married after all. I do so love a happy ending.'

'I'll send you a piece of wedding cake. Don't worry, I doubt Lauren would be baking it!'

'Okay, I'll keep you to that.'

From the kitchen, Beth could hear the group scraping back chairs. She really needed to get back to them. 'Sorry, I think I'm going to have to go — '

'Sure. I've kept you talking long enough . . . '

'No!' She hadn't meant that at all.

'Before you go . . . Beth, we never had the chance to say goodbye properly, did we . . . ?'

His voice was suddenly lower in tone, making her stomach turn somersaults. Tears began trickling down her face. But as long as she kept her voice steady, he'd never know. 'I'm not very good with goodbyes . . . '

'Then let's just say *arrivederci* instead. Beth?'

'*Arrivederci*, Roberto,' she whispered in return, as the course group clattered into the hall.

And she'd carried on saying it long after the call had ended, her throat feeling as dry as dust.

* * *

'Beth . . . ? Beth! Well? What do you think?'

While she'd been daydreaming, Lauren

275

had been busy. Beth looked up and straight into the full-length swing mirror that showed Lauren's stunning reflection. The ice-white wedding dress fitted perfectly around her petite frame and fell dramatically to the floor, the train puddling around her feet.

'Will I do?'

'Oh, Lauren! You'll do alright!' She could hardly speak for emotion. 'I'd give you a hug, but I don't want to crush the fabric.'

'I know what you mean. I might have to walk to the church, rather than squash into the car. I can't believe this is actually happening.' Lauren's voice wobbled, as Beth arranged her veil.

'There!' Beth arranged Lauren's cloud of golden hair so that the sapphire pendant Ewen had given her as a wedding gift was displayed to best advantage. That was if he had eyes for anything other than his beautiful bride's face when she lifted her veil.

'Shall we have a glass of champagne now?'

A bottle of the best vintage stood on the side table. The other twenty-three were waiting in the marquee in the garden for when the guests arrived back for the reception.

'It was a generous gesture from Roberto, wasn't it?' said Beth, feeling a frisson from just saying his name. She'd kept her promise to let him know that Lauren and Ewen's wedding was going ahead, but had never expected him to send such a generous gift.

Lauren raised her glass to Beth's. 'I told you he was a lovely man. Oh — !' She broke off, giggling and snorting. 'Bubbles up my nose! Wow, have you seen the time? You're not dressed yet, Beth. Talk about me running late!'

Beth fled from the room and back to her own, to slip into the ankle-length cream satin dress that Lauren had chosen for her. Not only was she Lauren's bridesmaid, she was also giving her away. Lauren seemed okay with her mother not coming over for the wedding because her mother's new husband wasn't in the best of health. Ewen had suggested that they spend some time in Australia during their honeymoon, and Beth could only hope that the visit would help in thawing Lauren's hitherto cool relationship with her mother.

Beth did one of her checks round, which included switching off the computer in the office. Every time she used it she was reminded of the garden pictures of her that Roberto had uploaded. She wished she had a personal picture of him. Not that she really needed one. He was in her head permanently, but the predominant image that seemed to have imprinted itself on her brain was of him tenderly carrying an injured Major through the pouring rain. Every night when she closed her eyes, she saw that.

The last thing left to do before leaving for the church was to tie a satin ribbon around Major's neck, because the dog was very much a part of the family and the ceremony. 'Sorry, boy, if you feel a sissy in this, but it's for Lauren. At least it's a blue ribbon!'

Taking a last look around the kitchen, it suddenly hit her how empty the Lodge was going to be from now on. Just her and Major. 'We're going to miss her, aren't we, boy?' she whispered. But there, she'd just have to get used to it, just like she was trying to get used to never seeing Roberto again. At least Lauren would only be living a few miles away, so she'd still see her often.

At the thought of Roberto, a tear slid down Beth's face, but she dashed it away. This was a day for happy tears only. Lauren's big day.

14

The inside of the church, with its pews, recesses and altar bedecked and scented with pink roses and mock orange blossom, had never looked lovelier. Nor had Lauren, as she glided down the aisle towards her groom. A smiling Ewen was equally impressive in immaculate top hat and tails.

Kevin took the ceremony and Beth tried hard not to cry as the vows were solemnly made. After the signing of the register, Beth, with Major at her side, followed the beaming Ewen and Lauren Walkis back down the aisle to the ringing of bells and traditional wedding music. Both sides were packed with the familiar faces of relatives and villagers, friends and neighbours; Ewen's parents, Pam and Derek Meadows, Jim the marquee helper, Fleur the vet . . .

And then there was Roberto.

Beth froze. It couldn't be. But it was. Roberto was standing at the back of the church and smiling at her. She couldn't make sense of it. She'd only had the one small glass of fizz!

Lauren turned to her, grinning. 'I invited him. Call it a wedding gift from me! It might have taken me a while to recognise true love in front of my own face,' she said, squeezing Ewen's hand, 'but I knew from the start there was something special between you and Roberto.'

At the doors, as the couple posed for the first photographs, Major dashed over to greet Roberto. Beth followed more slowly, still having trouble getting her legs to work.

'Hello there, boy, pleased to see me? Well aren't you the stylish one in your bow!'

'See,' said Beth, 'he hasn't forgotten you!' Roberto was no slouch in the style stakes either, wearing a beautifully cut navy suit, satin lapels to the jacket.

He moved forwards and embraced

her, his lips brushing each cheek in turn. His touch, his cologne, so achingly familiar. She longed to cling to him and stay that way forever.

Conscious of other guests having to swerve around them, she pulled away.

'Are you okay?' he asked.

'I think so,' she gulped. 'It's such a shock, seeing you here. I'd no idea Lauren had invited you.'

'It was very kind of her. And a good shock, I hope?'

She nodded dumbly.

He shook his head slightly, quizzically. 'You are pleased to see me, Beth?'

How could he doubt it? She gazed at him, willing him to read her thoughts. But then why should he have to. Perhaps it was the shock, but suddenly she was telling him.

'It seems like years since you left, Roberto. And I've missed you for every single second of them.'

He sighed, his shoulders relaxing. 'Oh, Beth, I've dreamt of you saying that. I would have come sooner, but first I had to make sure everything was settled before I — '

Kevin came up and pressed Roberto's arm. 'Nice to see you back in Shallingham, Mr Di Ferraio.'

'Thank you. Well, I did promise to come and take a look at the rood screen. I've not had a proper chance yet,' said Roberto, peering back into the church, 'but from here it looks *bellissimo.*'

Kevin beamed delightedly. 'I think I know what that means. But I can always ask Beth to translate. She's learning Italian at night classes.'

'Is she now!'

'Oh, dear, was it meant to be a surprise?' With a self-effacing grin, Kevin excused himself to speak with other guests.

Beth felt herself flush under Roberto's incisive gaze. She had started trying to learn the language, it was true, and she was enjoying the challenge. But it had been a bit of a double-edged sword. She'd thought it would make her feel closer to Roberto, though it had also served to remind her how distant he was — or so she'd imagined.

'How are you getting on with it?' he asked.

'Hmm. I might just be able to ask my way to the railway station!'

'You won't need to take the train when you visit Italy,' he said with a smile. 'I can drive you everywhere. Remember you said you'd like to see my mother's garden.'

Of course she did!

'Let me test you,' he said. Moving in close again, he began murmuring Italian phrases in her ear. She didn't have a clue what they meant, but his voice and nearness was having a chaotic effect on her senses.

'I'm sorry, I don't understand . . . '

'I was telling you why I had to come, Beth . . . my darling Beth . . . '

'Why?' she breathed.

'Because I couldn't stay away from you a minute longer. Because I believe — I hope — the time is right for us now.'

She gazed back at him wordlessly. Her heart was racing so hard she was surprised he couldn't hear it.

'I love you, Beth. I can't live without you.'

'Do you? Can't you?' She shook her head. She couldn't believe her ears, but she desperately wanted to believe.

'Do you think — ?' he faltered, uncharacteristically uncertain.

She held out her hands, and he caught them and held on them tightly.

'Do you think that now Lauren's married and settled and perhaps will not need you so much, that you might have space in your heart for someone who needs you very, very much?'

'Oh, Roberto!' she gasped, catching her lip, holding back a sob of pure joy. 'If only you knew how much I . . . I love you . . . '

The rest of her words were swept away as he enfolded her in an embrace which swung her round and completely off her feet.

She guessed they were causing a bit

of a spectacle when she heard someone's voice rise out of the melee of
guests. ' . . . well, you know what they
say — a wedding always leads to
another wedding!'

Roberto lowered her to the ground
and drew her to a quiet space outside
the church, but his arms didn't let go of
her. 'You will marry me, Beth?'

She gazed at him, loving him so
much, yet hardly able to speak. Despite
the midsummer sunshine, she shivered
delightedly, while Roberto waited, his
expression far from patient. She suddenly felt so light-hearted, her feet
hardly seemed to touch the ground.

'I love to see your smile,' he
murmured, 'but I hope you're laughing
with me, not at me!'

Confident of his love now, she
interlocked her fingers behind his neck
and drew his head down to meet hers in
a kiss. The look in his eyes quickly
turned to a longing that took her breath
away.

'Please, Beth, put me out of my

misery and marry me quickly.'

She laughed again. 'You'll have to wait until autumn. The marquee's booked up for the rest of the summer.'

He spluttered. 'Blow the marquee! If I have to, I'll grab Kevin and ask him to marry us right now. Or else I'll whisk you into the register office in Allsham.'

'How do you know there's a register office in Allsham!'

'I just happened to notice it the afternoon we went to shop and I made a mental note. Just in case it would come in useful one day!'

Her mouth opened and closed again. 'You can't have been thinking of marrying me then. You'd only known me a few hours.'

'I thought of it the first minute I saw you in the airport arrivals lounge.'

'You'll be telling me you believe in love at first sight next!' she teased. 'And I know you don't, because you told me emphatically enough.'

'Hmm . . . ' He gave a rueful grin. 'I did sound convincing, didn't I? I didn't convince myself for one second. I knew as soon as I saw you. Standing there looking all worried, determined, annoyed and . . . '

'Dishevelled,' she grimaced. 'In my dreadful gardening clothes.'

'And absolutely beautiful, that was what I was going to say. I didn't really notice what you were wearing, not until we got into the van, I think. I couldn't get my first impression of you out of my mind. You seemed to have an aura round your head, just like a wedding veil.'

'It must have been the airport lighting. Or you were just light-headed from the flight . . . ' She smiled, leaning into him, feeling so unbelievably happy.

'I've been light-headed ever since then! Although my practical side has been busy too, you know, working on plans for our future. I guess you wouldn't want to leave the Lodge or your garden after we're married. So I've set up a studio gallery in London so I can work from the UK. My Italian friend Leola and her English husband helped me there. They own a studio, and generously shared all their contacts to get me up and running as fast as possible.'

'I remember Leola,' Beth admitted. 'I was jealous.'

'Were you? I did wonder. I hoped. But not as insanely jealous as I was of Ewen that evening!'

Beth put her hands to her face briefly. 'When I think back to those two days . . . There was so much I wanted to tell you, but just couldn't.'

'I understand you had to keep your word to Lauren. I love you for your sense of family loyalty. I didn't know what to think half the time though, except that you seemed to dislike me rather a lot!'

'It was resistance, not dislike. Though I tried to!'

'Did you? You horror!' He caught her to him again. 'You seemed so welcoming to Luca at the airport, and ignored me.'

'I was so relieved to discover he was Lauren's Italian fiancé and not you.'

'And now I'm your Italian fiancé!'

He was, wasn't he!

'Come on,' she urged, tucking her arm through his. 'Lauren and Ewen are calling us over for the group photographs.'

'I'll have to get used to being on the posing side of the lens,' he said. 'Next time it'll be at our wedding!'

And as the camera flashed, Roberto's dark eyes met hers head-on. It was a look that Beth was already getting used to. The look of love.

THE END